IN ROAST MORTEM

A ROASTWOOD HOLLOW COZY MYSTERY
BOOK 1

KRISTIN HELLING

Time to get cozy!

IN ROAST MORTEM
by Kristin Helling

ISBN-13: 978-1-946921-47-5

ADRENALINE

Wordwraith Books, LLC
705-B SE Melody Lane #149
Lee's Summit, MO 64063
e-mail *wordwraiths@gmail.com*
website *www.wordwraiths.com*
Edited by Midwrite Editorial www.midwrite.com
Cover Design by DLR Cover Designs www.
dlrcoverdesigns.com
Kristin's email *author@kristinhelling.com*
Kristin's website *kristinhelling.com*
The Library of Congress Cataloging-in-Publication Data
is available upon request.

BOOKS BY KRISTIN HELLING

THE IDEA MAN TRILOGY
(comedic, suspense thriller)

The Idea Man

The Marked Man

The True Man

THE MASTERMIND MURDERERS SERIES
(psychological, crime thriller)

The Altruism Effect

The Bystander Effect

The Carbon Effect

The Domino Effect

STANDALONE BOOKS
(psychological, crime thriller)

Capsule

(psychological, action adventure Thriller)

The Severed Sea

COZY MYSTERY SERIES

In Roast Mortem

More to come…

For Austin, Remy, and Cozette.

For PVCH.

And for good espresso.

CHAPTER
ONE

Clementine Matthews adjusted the stainless steel lever on the side of the roaring machine, shifting the airflow inside the coffee roaster as she neared the first crack. This was the point in the roasting process where the endothermic heat inside the beans switched to exothermic, then *crack!* Like popcorn. She pushed her fiery orange hair off her shoulder, tracked her time on the clipboard, then pocketed the permanent marker in her denim apron.

As she'd done hundreds of times before, she pulled the sample trier out of the face of the roaster and held it up to the lamp above, studying the color of the beans as the vapors wafted under her nose. The sound of the beans snapped and popped through the exposed hole left by the trier.

"What'd you say, Ro? Think they're in first crack?" She looked over at Robusta's favorite spot in the roastery, a stack of wooden pallets by the window, but her ivory and red bearded dragon wasn't perched there. Bearded dragons were social and intuitive creatures, and Clem often brought Ro along when she came to the roastery alone in the evenings. Although quiet, the reptile's presence was good company.

Clem cocked her brow, though it wasn't unusual for Robusta to wander around from time to time, if she'd heard a noise that Clementine couldn't hear over the motor of the roasting drum.

"Ahh, you know I can't leave the roaster unattended when beans are cooking!" she called out again, turning her attention back to the drum. Robusta was probably just exploring the back room of the roastery, trying to see if there were any spare crickets for a snack.

Clem checked the development of the beans once more. The vapors had picked up, escaping out of the top of the hopper funnel. There was always a point in the roast where it did this, but she thought she'd better go take a quick peek at the chimney to make sure the vapors stayed a light, whitish gray. If they turned black, that was a bad sign there may be a fire inside the chimney. Not something that happened often, if ever, but ducting fires could happen.

She secured the trier back into its hole and rushed to the door, peddling up the stairs in her black Vans. She backed up in the parking lot, catching sight of the chimney on the roof, a white vapor billowing from the rain cap of the ducting. Perfect. Right where she needed to be. She started towards the roastery door when a movement caught her peripheral vision.

Dread and panic washed over her at the sight of the door to the back room of the roastery swinging open. She ran over and slammed the heavy metal door closed from the outside, then scanned the vicinity.

Robusta could easily blend in with the surrounding weeds, native vegetation, and the sandy-colored gravel pathway that led from one door to the other to the parking lot. However, the little reptile was wearing a black Jurassic Park hoodie made from one of Clementine's socks, which made her easier for Clem to spot.

She instantly regretted that she had slammed the door closed out of instinct, because it was always locked on the outside.

Locked on the outside ... did that mean who-ever opened it, opened it from the inside? Had she been inside roasting the whole time, not alone?

Was it smart for her to then burst into the roastery and shout out for Robusta, if someone had been lurking? Most definitely not.

She couldn't leave Ro inside though. Clem had to see if she was in there to begin with before she searched the outside in a frenzy.

Shoving all apprehension to the back of her mind, she rushed back to the main entrance, charging down the short stairs. The beans clanked inside the roaster unnoticed, forgotten.

"Robusta!" she yelled out, gasping as the little bearded dragon emerged from the back room, trotting slowly and lifting her legs in an exaggerated fashion. "There you are." She exhaled, bending down, and scooping her up. As she lifted Robusta, a smudge of crimson swiped her hand. Her stomach knotted as she lifted Robusta to look at her claws, then her gaze fell to the floor, where a trail of bearded dragon tracks in what appeared to be red paint led from the back room.

A quick thought surfaced that perhaps someone had been painting. But it didn't smell like paint. It smelled metallic.

4

Blood.

"Are you hurt?" She chirped, her throat tightening. There was only one thing she could do next.

Follow the trail.

It took everything to force her heavy legs forward into the back room. She clutched Robusta to her chest and opened her mouth to scream, but the air had been knocked out of her.

There, in a pool of blood, lay a body, a knife sticking out of his gut.

It was the lifeless form of the one person who had a key to that backroom door. He wasn't in the roasting facility trying to go out. He was outside and used his own key to get in.

It was the owner of the building. Her landlord, Paul Wright.

Not even the smell of the coffee could mask the stench. The sight was nauseating. She needed to get out of there. Now.

Clutching Robusta, Clementine spun around and rushed out of the room. She leaped over the trail of bloody reptile tracks and into the main room, searching for her phone to call for help, the logical next step.

She snatched her phone from where it lay by the cart of pre-measured green beans next to the roaster. In a shaken panic, she pulled the lever to drop the beans into the rotating cooling bin.

They spun.

Burnt to a crisp.

CHAPTER
TWO

Clementine crinkled the foil blanket tighter around her shoulders as she sat in the back of the ambulance. She'd already had her vitals checked, even though she'd tried to refuse it. She was okay, but they kept telling her she was experiencing shock.

Paul Wright, her landlord, however, was not okay. They wheeled him out of the roasting facility in a zipped-up body bag: a black one, like the movies. The building was swarmed with police, paramedics, and even a fire truck. Nothing ever happened in the small town of Roastwood Hollow more than a smoking trash can from someone failing to extinguish their cigarette butt.

"You really should eat something," Josie, who ran the coffeehouse side of the business, said as she handed Clem a snack wrapped in tissue paper. "I brought you a protein oat ball from the shop."

Clementine took it and tried a small bite of the protein ball, one side of the foil blanket falling from her shoulder. She nodded as a thank you, unable to mumble the words.

"Ms. Matthews?"

She turned her head, finishing a swallow of oats and peanut butter.

"My name is Officer Drake. Do you have a moment to speak?"

She did not recognize him as a regular Roastwood Hollow policeman. Clem was familiar with most of the cops around here, not only because this was a small town, but because many of them frequented the coffee-house in the mornings for their cup of joe. Though, she had heard that this town was a training precinct. A lot of officers were sent here straight out of the academy to learn the ropes before heading to their permanent cities to work.

"Can't she just have a rest for a minute? She's already been bombarded with questions since she called this in." Josie spoke up; her presence was bold.

Clementine didn't need a protector; she could hold her own, but it was nice to have someone who wasn't afraid to speak up, especially when it came to customer service at the shop. Josie was always quick on her feet, ready with a reply to diffuse the situation.

"No, sorry, we need to speak to Ms. Matthews now, before too much time has passed. It's better to get a statement when the crime has first happened. Time can easily skew someone's memory."

Clementine nodded and looked over at Josie. "Can you take Ro back home for me?" Clem lifted Robusta and kissed her on the scaly head, then held her out in her harness with a leash. Josie took Robusta with no hesitation and took off.

Clementine turned to the officer, who looked confused at her behavior toward her reptile. In happier times, she might have teased him about it: had he never seen a bearded dragon on a harness before? Or perhaps, never one in a sock hoodie? But the heavy feeling of dread in the pit of her stomach did not lend to much joking.

"Do you need me to get down?" she asked, looking over her black jeans and Vans at the gravel below.

"No, you can stay seated there, I just have a few questions."

Clem shifted on the edge of the ambulance. The officer, or PI, or whoever he was, looked like he could be her age, if not younger. That was the thing about nearing the end of her twenties. The other people in her generation were in the same season of life, and that included being in career jobs. Doctors, dentists, and mail carriers all tended to be the same age as her, instead of older.

"Can you explain what happened when you found the body?"

"You mean Paul? When I found Paul?" she asked, biting her lip at her outburst. The poor guy was just doing his job. But he had to understand what she'd just gone through.

"Of course. And I understand that you've already explained it to dispatch, and again to the first responders, but it's protocol we ask again."

A somber wave hit her like a tsunami. She hadn't felt like crying this entire time. Crying was not her first instinct. She'd rather be stone-faced and cold, get through the situation, and then let her emotion do what it wanted when she was in the privacy of her apartment.

Though the moment she thought about it, her eyes stung. "Well..." She cleared her throat. A drink of water to wash down the peanut butter would have been welcome. "I was catching up on roasting for some clients' orders—"

"Do you often come here at night?"

Taken aback by his interruption, she

stammered through a dry throat, "I mean, yeah. And no. I don't make it a habit, but sometimes I get behind, so I needed to come. And it wasn't night exactly, I mean, sevenish."

"Alone?"

"I had Robusta with me."

"Your friend?" He had his small spiral notebook out, scratching onto its surface. He brought the pen up to his mouth and bit the end of it in thought.

She cocked an eyebrow. She thought it'd be more effective if he used his phone to record their conversation, but she wasn't about to tell him how to do his job.

"My beardie—" She cleared her throat. "Bearded dragon."

He lowered the pen as he looked back up at her. "Ah, right."

She thought she'd caught a hint of a smile on his face. She brushed it off with an eye roll that he wouldn't see anyway, because his nose was back in his notebook.

"And you just... walked in on the body? On Paul?"

She traced along the stitching of her pants with her index finger. "Yeah. I was in the middle of a roast, and Robusta went wandering again. So when I went to go check on her...is when I found Paul."

He nodded. "And were you current on your rent?"

She almost choked on her saliva. "Yes." There was no question about that. "Why is that relevant?"

"Just getting all the facts, ma'am."

Ma'am? Did he just call her ma'am? They likely graduated in the same class year, and he was addressing her as though she were his elder. Ma'am was so outdated. Was he a country boy? There were only so many options why he'd use this title when he most definitely knew her name.

She'd probably been taking too long to respond. Or, did he ask her another question that she didn't hear while her mind reeled over being called ma'am? A pang rippled in her stomach when it occurred to her that, perhaps, she was the number one suspect. She cleared her throat again.

"Wait, you don't... you don't think I have anything to do with this, do you? Paul was my landlord. We had a great professional relationship. Why would I kill him?"

"You tell me."

She scoffed. "I'm not a murderer. I couldn't even stand to look at the blood. I don't even know if I'll be able to get over this enough to come back to work!" She swiped her sweaty palms on her black jeans, hoping he hadn't noticed them tremble.

"We must rule out all the options. And you were alone in the building. And usually, the victim knows the murderer personally."

"Everyone knows everyone in this town!" She put her head into her hands, feeling flushed. She needed to calm herself. With the stereotypes that usually came with redheads, tempers, and tattoos, she didn't need to lean into her own cliché.

The officer quietly scrawled into the notebook, which infuriated her even more.

She took a deep breath. "Look, I'm willing to work with you and tell you anything you need to know. I'm not withholding information. We got off on the wrong foot. I want you to search the facility up and down. I'm afraid to work here while there is a murderer on the loose."

This was true, but other concerns surfaced that she hadn't considered amid the shock of the situation. Concerns like, what happens when the owner of the building you rent turns up dead? Would her business be kicked out? Could she fit her roaster into the coffeehouse and share space with Josie, if she had to? Thirteen hundred pounds of solid cast iron wasn't easy to move. What about Paul's family? She tried to keep her mind from spiraling out of control.

"Uhm, if you look at my roast logs, you will see the exact time that I was doing a batch. When you are running a batch, you cannot leave the roaster unattended. With the batch size that I had, my profile was 18 minutes." She took another shaky breath, watching his expression as he analyzed her statement.

"And the door on the side of the building that leads to that back room; it wasn't open when you got here this evening?"

"No, not that I remember. I would have noticed it. I always have a heightened sense of awareness when I'm here by myself. With Robusta."

"Hm. But you didn't notice when your lizard—"

"Bearded dragon."

"Right, uh, when your pet wandered off?"

She assumed he was referring to the tracks in the pool of blood. Flashes of the crime scene kept appearing in her mind just as she'd shake them away. She tried to remain focused. She had to clear her name so they could figure out who actually did this, get them away from her town, and bring that sense of safety back to Roastwood Hollow.

"It's not unusual for her to explore the

roasting facility while I work. She likes to find bugs for a snack."

The officer furrowed his brow and nodded. "And you say you didn't hear any commotion while you were working?"

She shook her head. "The roaster is quite loud while in operation. I didn't hear anyone come in. And…" She held back a gag. "…the smell. I don't imagine it's like that when the person is just killed."

He reached into his pocket and pulled out a cell phone, reading a message and then looking up at her again. "Do you have security cameras that we can pull footage from? One of the investigators says he saw a camera in the rafters of the main room."

She swallowed hard, racking her mind. "I do have a camera in the main room over my roaster, but it only notifies me of motion detected when the place is locked up."

"How convenient."

She laughed nervously under her breath at his near-offensive sarcasm. "No, definitely not… convenient." She responded quietly, looking at the abandoned protein ball next to her on the floor of the ambulance. She wasn't hungry anyway.

Clementine pushed the foil blanket off her shoulders and gingerly got down off the back of the ambulance. The officer put his arm out to assist her, but she saw it too late and was fine getting down on her own anyway. She couldn't get a good read on him. At times he seemed suspicious of her, and at others it appeared like he wanted to protect her. The hot and cold nature of his behavior was exhausting. Or maybe that was just because it had been a long night after a roasting shift, which always seemed more physically demanding than she'd planned for. Lifting twenty-pound buckets of raw green coffee overhead to the roaster hopper over and over was not for the weak.

"Did you have any other questions for me, Officer...Drake?" She caught the name tag on his uniform, as she couldn't remember what he'd said earlier. When he'd introduced himself, it went in one ear and out the other.

"Uh, no Ms. Matthews. I'll go ahead and take your information down so that we can reach back out to you if anything surfaces."

"The paramedics took my info earlier if you want to swap notes?" She skirted around a snarky tone, trying not to sound disrespectful. "Kidding. I'll give it to you. Oh, I wanted to ask. What... happens next? To Paul? He was my landlord and... I have a lot of thoughts running through my mind." She reached into her back pocket to retrieve her license once more and handed it over.

Simon Drake took the ID, marking information down in his pad, then raised his eyebrow. "About losing the building for your business?"

She took the notebook. "Oh god, well yes. I mean… I do want to know that as well, but … " She let out a shaky breath. "I meant with his…body and his family. Hopefully you've reached out to them? And not only that, but I mean… a killer is on the loose. Am I safe here?" She pinched the bridge of her nose.

"His family has been notified, yes. And an autopsy has been requested, which is common in cases like this. I wouldn't come here by yourself in the meantime, if that's what you're asking. But we are on it. And maybe update your cameras to record more than just potential motion at night." He pocketed his phone, notebook, and pen, then nodded. Simon spun on his heels and walked back toward the other officers emerging from the building.

It was like a band-aid had been ripped off when he walked away; Clem was stunned by a moment of sudden unwelcome loneliness. Now what? She was cleared to leave by the paramedics. She was fine physically.

She was *fine*. Right?

Of course, it occurred to her that she was the first suspect, having been the one that discovered the body. And she had no alibi, because the body had been found in the location of her alibi. Unless the police took her roasting profile timing stuff seriously. She *did* have the logs for that. She wouldn't have had time to doctor them. And Robusta, the only other witness, was no help.

The authorities said they would lock up the building when they left; the building that had all her business assets inside it. The crime scene.

She turned to go to her car, but her legs were heavy and unstable. The scene of Paul lying in a pool of his own blood made her queasy. She was always teased about her dizziness at the sight of blood: that it was linked to her ginger hair.

"Hey, uhhh!" She yelled out as another officer neared the building.

He turned to face her, his push-broom mustache square in the center of his face.

She rocked back on her heels. "Can you or another officer perhaps give me a ride home? I can come back and get my car later. I just... I don't want to have to call my friend to come back and get me. I could call an Uber—"

"I'll take you," Simon called over to his partner. "I'll take her," he confirmed.

Her eyes darted over to Officer Drake, taken aback by his eagerness, but also grateful for his willingness. Was his motivation to be kind? Get more time with her to ask more questions and gauge that she wasn't a killer? The thought of more questions brought apprehension; however, that was in her favor perhaps.

Plus, he wasn't too bad to look at, with his carefree brunette hair and dark eyes. And she wasn't in any condition to drive. And she could use the company.

CHAPTER
THREE

Clementine ducked into the passenger seat of the cop cruiser and buckled her seat belt as Simon closed her door and walked around the front. Through the windshield, she saw him shout something to another officer. Part of her felt like she should stay while there were emergency vehicles at her roasting facility, and to lock up at the end. But they insisted after hours of questioning her, and with it getting dark, that she should go home. She did not argue; her support system had gone home with Josie, and all Clem wanted to do was cuddle up with Robusta.

Simon waved and opened the driver's side, hopping in.

She gave him her address again, holding her tongue that she'd already given it to him and his comrades multiple times, and they drove away from the roasting facility. She watched the blur of the emergency vehicle lights in the rearview mirror. She just wanted to sit in silence, but the inevitable was impending.

"So what's with the reptile?" he asked, casually.

It bothered her that this was just another day of work for him. She cleared her throat. "Uh, Robusta is my bearded dragon. She's my pet. My best friend. She's more social than you would think. But I guess you have to be a *reptile* person to understand. And her name comes from a coffee term. A species of a coffee plant. "

"Why not a cat or a dog?" he asked.

She humored him. He was just trying to make small talk so that the car ride wasn't awkward. Because it indeed was awkward. At least she was in the front seat riding tandem with him and not in the back behind the bars.

"Bearded dragons are less high maintenance. Apart from feeding her and providing a comfortable habitat, she's pretty self-sufficient. She isn't needy for attention like a dog, and I'm allergic to cats. If my throat didn't close when I was within a small radius of cats, I'd likely go that route." She shrugged, then crossed her arms over her chest.

"I see…" he concluded.

"Are you… new to Roastwood Hollow?" she asked. She already knew the answer. He was nice enough to be willing to take her home, and if small talk was what he wanted, small talk was what he was going to get.

"Uh, yes. It's a training precinct. So I will most likely be assigned to a different metro city as soon as I learn the ropes here. I'm right out of the academy now, my first time in the field. Of course, most officers don't like to admit that. But my dad has been a police officer my entire life. I followed in his footsteps. I always knew it was what I wanted to do, even though my mom wasn't too keen when I got serious about it."

"Oh?"

"Yeah well, it isn't the safest profession. I tell her she's lucky—at least I didn't enlist."

"Seems like you have pretty great parents." She was quiet for a moment, then words escaped her mouth before her brain had time to protest. "Cops aren't necessarily everyone's favorite right now." She avoided his gaze.

"You don't say?"

She laughed. With her elbow propped on the arm rest, she covered her mouth with the back of her hand.

He sighed and used the turn signal at the

corner. "I try to just be a good human, and not fall into the traps other officers sometimes can. I don't feed that fire. Because there are some dangerous ones, no doubt."

She nodded. It was an important conversation to have, but she respected his response. "I appreciate that you didn't get defensive when I brought that up. Not that you have to prove anything to me." She looked over and saw his lips curve into a small smile.

He followed the GPS directions, turning the volume down on the police radio receiver to hear the navigation voice. She drifted into a daydream as the traffic lights and street lamps went past in a blurry haze. She was truly exhausted, and it was just now hitting her. She slumped in the seat, head swaying, eyelids drooping.

"How about you?"

"Huh?" she asked.

"Why did you decide to go into coffee?"

She paused for a moment and let the question sink in. "It was almost by accident. I was graduating college and needed a job. Josie told me they needed help. So I started over at the cafe as a barista. I just fell in love with it. There's such an art and a science to it. So much more than people who pick up their morning cup of coffee can even understand. I love the global closeness of the craft, and connecting with the people who grow it. I also love not only the roasting process, but the process of brewing it too, for people to enjoy and connect over. It's not just a drink, you know?"

Despite her exhaustion, the words flicked off her tongue as if second nature.

"That's really cool," he said quietly, seeming to absorb her words. "And you own Roastwood Coffee?"

"Uh, yeah. I own fifty percent: the roasting side. We were buying beans from somewhere else until we realized that we could do it ourselves. My partner Josie owns the other half, the coffee shop half."

"Oh! The friend who took your lizard home?"

She laughed. *Bearded dragon. Forget it.* "Yeah, that's Josie."

A silence swept the car once more as they turned onto her street. "My apartment is right up there, but you can let me out here."

He pulled up a little bit in the parking lot and eased to a stop.

"Thank you for not making me sit in the back seat," she joked, still feeling a little uncomfortable, but she couldn't help it. He laughed.

So the effort for the joke was worth it. "I'm sorry, I make jokes when I don't know what else to say. It's probably inappropriate considering what… happened tonight." The lump in her throat reemerged. She put her hand on the door handle.

"I understand." He offered her a soft smile.

It seemed genuine.

"Thank you for the ride, Officer Drake."

"Simon's fine."

She nodded. Then she pushed open the door to the cool air. "Bye." The word was raspy in her throat.

"Hey, do you have your phone on you?" he asked quickly.

"Yeah, I do. Why?"

"Can I see it?"

She wrinkled her brow, pulling her cell from her back pocket and handing it to him.

He typed something into it and handed the phone back to her as quickly as she'd given him it. "I just put my number in there. If you need anything at all, reach out okay? I mean, if you remember something from earlier tonight, or just anything."

She could tell he was trying to keep it professional, but it was also a kind gesture. "Thanks."

"Have a good night, Ms. Matthews."

"You too. And… Clem is fine." She closed the door to the cop car and headed toward her apartment in haste, pulling her keys out of her other pocket and fumbling with them until she reached her door.

CHAPTER
FOUR

Clementine wrapped her black fingernails tightly around the warm to-go cup as she walked down the cobblestone sidewalk toward the town meeting hall. She wasn't feeling very confident, her breath shallow and punchy. She hadn't been around people in a couple of weeks, isolating at home to take some time away from work.

Josie had told her to take some time off, and that she'd make sure to warn her when they started to get low on beans. Luckily, Clem had been keeping a generous backstock, in case she got sick or wanted to go on vacation. In this case, the unforeseen circumstances of her absence warranted using most, if not all, of it.

She had gotten used to lounging on the

couch in her fuzzy socks, Robusta on her lap. It was much needed time away from the roasting facility, where her dreams took her often. She would doze off, only to rush awake, tearing herself away from images of the roastery filling with syrupy blood.

She approached the meeting hall and pulled open the door. A bell dinged as she entered. The ambient crowd noise dropped to hushed tones—unless she was only imagining it. She pursed her lips and nodded hello at a few of the eyes that wandered her direction.

"Clem! You came!" Polly, the executive director of their small-town district, approached her.

"Yes, of course. It's our monthly meeting. Why wouldn't I be here?" She worried she came off accusatory. Polly was being sweet, and quite frankly, the only person brave enough to approach her.

"Well, you know. You've been through so much. Nobody expected you to be ready to be out again...Here take a seat next to me, it's open. Here's an itinerary."

Clementine smiled softly at her. Polly was able to talk fast and sometimes not able to stop talking when she was nervous. Clem sat down in the folding chair and wiggled her seat closer to the table. She looked over the room, her eyes resting on the Mr. Coffee pot spawned from the '90s, most likely with brewed canned coffee grounds also from the '90s. She reached out and pulled her own coffee cup closer to her chest. A plethora of people from the town showed up for this meeting. Roastwood Hollow held them once a month, which Clementine felt was probably a bit too much.

Even after her defensive response towards Polly, she debated whether or not she would come today. She definitely didn't feel like engaging in gossip with the others in this small town. And there was plenty of it.

"Alright, everyone, welcome!" The voice of the president of their small historic downtown organization rang out.

Clementine sank deeper in her chair, relieved by the announcement to start the meeting, giving little time for others to approach her for small talk. She'd planned out her arrival time perfectly.

Polly nodded to the president and then took the reins as she normally would. "Usually, when we see new faces, we like to go around the room and introduce ourselves. But we have a lot to go over today, so we're going to go ahead and skip that this time. Please feel free to hang back afterwards and meet your fellow community members at the end."

Clementine resisted the urge to make any celebratory noises towards this statement.

"We're going to start with the Roastwood Hollow police before we get into other things. Thank you for attending, Captain Jones."

He nodded, push-broom mustache and all.

Clementine shifted in her seat, crossing her ankles and bouncing them back and forth under the table.

He grumbled, "I don't have much to report. Just... lock your cars and close your garage doors. Most crime that happens in our neck of the woods is failure of residents due diligence in locking their cars and closing their garage doors."

His heavy southern drawl was enough to make her fall asleep, though this was the part of the meeting where she wanted to hang onto his every word. Was he going to mention anything about the case?

"Right. Thank you, Captain." Polly shuffled her papers. "Very sound advice. Lock your doors, people." She smiled sweetly as she dragged her pen over the itinerary. "Do we have a representative here from the city development and planning department?" She looked up over her cat eye glasses.

A pang of nerves shocked Clem into attention. Wait, he's not going to say anything about the case? And nobody else is either.

Would it be smart for her to bring it up? There was enough attention on her as a suspect already: all of the judging looks and prying neighbors. Before she could muster the courage to speak up, the vice president of the association leaned over and whispered something into Polly's ear. Polly straightened her spine and adjusted in her seat.

"Before we move on, Captain, folks are wanting to know if you have any more information concerning ..." She cleared her throat. "Mr. Wright's accident?"

Clementine relaxed for a moment, relieved Polly brought it up so she didn't have to. Wait, *accident*? What in the actual hell? Her gut filled with rage. They weren't there. They didn't see it like she did. Sure, they could speculate, but nobody saw the pool of blood around her landlord. Those who really knew Paul would know that was no accident. Regardless of how many times the crime scene cleaning crew scrubbed the floor in her back room, she'd never unsee it.

She came out of her memory as the captain began quickly. "It's an ongoing investigation, and I know folks are nervous, but there is nothing to worry about. There's no killer on the loose. Paul's death was tragic, and the family is only asking for peace."

Clementine wasn't sure if she imagined it

or not, but eyes seemed to avoid her, as though they didn't want to look anywhere close to her direction.

"What of the building, sir?" one of the other residents asked.

Her throat constricted. That's nobody's business! *She* didn't even have that information.

"Next of kin is deciding what to do, whether they'll continue leasing, or sell."

Her cheeks were hot. Her heart knocked inside her chest. This was no accident. Was the captain just telling the townspeople this to keep them from panic? Did they actually have a ton of things going on behind the scenes that they wouldn't tell the general public? Or…

Her mind conjured up the worst. They'd had enough time in her absence to get autopsy results back. Had they truly deemed it an accident?

There was a pause in the room, before Polly spoke up again. "Thank you, Captain Jones. Now if there is no city development and planning rep available, we need to move on to discussing the Snowflake Festival taking place this next weekend. I have already reached out to the vendors, and we are just waiting to hear back from two organizations on their sponsorships for the fireworks. Peggy, have you heard back from the hospital yet on their donation?"

It took all of Clementine's restraint to remain seated in her flimsy folding chair. She was done with these people. Nobody cared about what happened to Paul. They only cared about gossiping, and when no gossip was to be had, or wasn't interesting or new enough anymore, they channeled all of their energy into planning the next town festival, as though the crime never even happened. It was like they were both avoiding her and prying into her business at the same time. The room spun.

She pushed back her chair. It screeched across the linoleum floor.

Polly's gaze shot to her.

"Bathroom?" Clem mouthed at her.

Polly nodded and continued addressing the room, next about busing in children for the singing choir that would be attending the Snowflake Festival.

Clementine patted her face with cool water from the bathroom faucet. She rested her hands on both sides of the sink and peered up at the mirror, into her pale face. She thought back to all the times she'd disputed with her landlord, Paul. He was your typical business-man, and whenever there were leaks or issues with the building, he tended to prioritize everything else over what she needed fixed. Sure, she could go ahead and fix it by herself, but then that came out of Roastwood Coffee's budget, and she already paid rent for the place. When there was leaking in the roof on or near her coffee roaster—a machine that lit-erally cost more than anything she'd ever pur-chased in her entire life—she fumed when he hadn't made that a priority. But that surely didn't count as a motive for murder, and even though Paul was the worst from time to time, he didn't deserve to be murdered either. And he definitely deserved a thorough investiga-tion into his untimely death. It was no accident.

Clem sat through the rest of the meeting, bouncing her crossed ankles under the table and biting off any length of her black-painted fingernails she had left. The remainder of the meeting itinerary was a blur. She'd typically attend these meetings to see what was going on in the town, and stay up to date on events in case they'd affect her business. Social media hits on the town's website and which vendors were booked for the Snowflake Festival were the furthest matters of importance on her mind.

She suspected that she would hear from Paul's family soon enough. Perhaps, instead of spending time sitting in this useless meeting, she should be in her roastery, packing up all the things for her business because she was going to need to find another place to roast. What were the odds that the family wouldn't sell the building and that they'd continue renting to her? If they didn't reach out to her soon, she'd reach out to them. She still had a couple of years on her lease yet, and first right of refusal if they sold, which was on her side. Though it was nobody here's business. The meeting adjourned and Clem moved to stand, but not before reaching for her coffee, even if it was no longer warm.

"It's like they don't even care," Clem heard behind her. She whipped around to see Michael standing there. He owned a clothing boutique a few stores up from the cafe, selling mostly local goods and locally branded t-shirts. She narrowed her eyes. He was in the crowd of those who didn't care. He could have spoken up. Then again, everyone could have been intimidated by the captain of the police. She couldn't wait to talk to Simon again, to see if they really had brushed off the case and closed it as a suicide, or if the captain was just spewing that at the meeting so people in the town would back off.

"It does feel that way, doesn't it?" she said to Michael under her breath, gathering the itinerary papers.

"Have the Wrights reached out to you yet about your lease?" he asked.

"They haven't. Have they reached out to you?" That was what she had in common with Michael. Paul owned more than just her building in the town—he was also Michael's landlord.

"Not yet, but I'm not too worried, honestly. I know his wife has some properties of her own. Unless they sell, they'll likely just carry the lease." He shrugged, pushing his black-framed glasses back up the bridge of his nose.

"I wouldn't be too sure. If your loved one was killed in your own building, would you keep it?"

Michael bit his bottom lip thoughtfully for a moment. "Good point."

"You could buy it." She backed up from her chair as though unclaiming it. The closer she could get to the door and avoid any other conversations, the better.

"Ha! I struggled to make rent most months with my sales, let alone being able to buy the building, or multiple buildings, for that matter."

She was mostly joking. But she was in that same boat. Now that the police seemed to have crossed her off their suspect list, perhaps she could look into it. According to the captain, it appeared they'd crossed off everyone but the victim. She could talk to the Wrights, and even visit the bank about the possibility of a loan. She'd never tried it before, hadn't even considered that idea with her mind so cloudy. It could be worth a shot.

"How are you holding up, kid?" he asked her.

She gave a small smile. Had he noticed her trance? He seemed genuine, unlike the rest of the Nosy Nellys in that room: some of whom she was certain were eavesdropping right then. "You know…" she responded, knowing if she said she was okay, it wouldn't come out right. "Everything is up in the air with my future. Someone innocent is dead. And uhhh, yeah." She trailed off. She almost said something about being sick and tired of all the gossip in this town. But she didn't want to make herself even more of a target than she already was.

"Welp, look at the time. I'm about to open the store. Catch you later." Michael saluted her, two fingers to his forehead, and took off with his binder tucked under his arm.

Clementine nodded, jolted by the sudden departure, but also grateful. She stole a quick glance around the room at those who were left. The quilting shop ladies, the one private citizen that liked to come to these meetings just to hear what was going on and perhaps volunteer, the American Legion retirees, reps from the city, from the university, from the Economic Development Council, the business owners. And then there was Polly, the executive director.

Perhaps she should stick around and talk to Polly. The executive director knew everyone. She was friendly with the chief of police, the police captain, and the fire marshal. She knew who to talk to when raising funding, who drove what cars, who parked where, all the rumors, new people moving in, business owners wanting to expand, ones who didn't have the proper permits. Everything. Polly was definitely one to be everywhere and know everyone. The eyes and ears of Roastwood Hollow. Was she there the evening that Paul was killed? Oftentimes, Polly was sprucing flowers or picking up trash, or visiting the local restaurants. Perhaps Clementine needed to question her about that. Of course, she didn't think Polly could hurt a fly.

Perhaps Polly knew something about the case more than Clementine did, which is why she didn't press the captain further on the issue. Yes, she needed to talk to Polly.

Clem stood off to the side of the group of three ladies continuing to discuss the Snowflake festival.

"I want to purchase large letters that spell out the word 'merry'. It's a great photo op and we could put it in the park across the street from the shops." Diane held her phone up to show the others.

"Oh, the park the carolers cross through?" Polly marked something down on her notebook and turned back to the group.

"Yes, exactly. Polly, are there funds in the budget for purchasing the letters instead of renting this year?"

"Let me get back to you on that, but I see it as a clear possibility."

"I know neighboring towns have done that —oh hello Clementine! Are you going to be providing the coffee for the event again this year?" Christie, the event space owner, chimed in.

Polly and Diane backed up the circle for Clementine to be included. She smiled shyly and cleared her throat, awkwardly swinging her foot back and forth before joining the circle.

"Yea… yeah. I was planning on having a tent with hot coffee and hot chocolates for the kids."

"Excellent!"

"Anything is better than… well—" Diane looked down at her styrofoam cup of coffee from the legion. "Don't tell Joe though…" The whole circle laughed.

Clem smiled. *Don't tell so and so.* Famous last words. Someone always told someone here. Of course, that could also be used to her advantage at certain times. "I was hoping to have a word with Polly?"

"Yes, I was on my way out anyway. Thank you ladies. Diane, I'll email you about the budget." They said their goodbyes, and Polly led Clementine to the door with her hand on the small of her back.

"How are you, sweetie? I know that must have been tough, sitting and listening to that. I was sure to get it moving along so we didn't dwell so much on it."

Clementine's cheeks burned. Polly could be so dense sometimes. "I almost didn't come, if that answers your question," she said softly. She wasn't malicious, and she tried to smooth her upper brow, the one her mom told her furrowed when she was frustrated. "It just happened so soon. I'd like to get back to some kind of normalcy though, ya know? I'm heading to the roastery after this for the first time since it happened. I just need… to get back to doing what I was doing, and the team at the shop are getting close to running out of the supply of beans we had there. So really, I have no choice."

"Have you gotten a chance to talk with Paul's family yet? I spoke with Michael and he wasn't sure about the fate of the buildings. And the city said nothing has come through their end yet."

Polly did know everything.

"No, not yet, but would you let me know first if you hear anything?" Clem asked. Keeping Polly on her side was smart. "Polly?" She thought she'd shoot her shot.

"Yeah, sweetie?" She grabbed Clementine's bicep and gave it a gentle squeeze, leaning in.

Clem followed suit, leaned in and spoke quieter. "Were you… there that night? The night Paul… died."

Polly's puff painted, holiday sweatshirt, shoulders dropped. "I was, sweetie."

Clem took a deep breath.

"But I saw nothing. I was over at the event space with Christie, helping her handle the indoor lighting. I didn't see anybody coming or going on your side of the street. I would have told the police if I had. And sweetie, it's

not worth looking into. Paul's gone, by suicide. We know that now. There's nothing to
worry about."

"But maybe they told us that to make us
feel falsely secure. Maybe they got it wrong?"
she pushed further.

"Clementine, I suggest you move on." Polly's voice changed. It was stiff and did not
waiver.

Clem felt the hairs on her arms prick up.
"Okay," she said quickly, shutting it down.
What a weird interaction. Perhaps there was
something more there, but she didn't want to
press it, because she needed to be on Polly's
good side. She needed her knowledge.
"Thank you," Clem said, pursing her lips.
"That helps... me a lot. I'll let it go." She
smiled, fake albeit; she could play the game.

"I really appreciate you offering the coffee
for the Snowflake Festival. I did hear a rumor
that the Boy Scouts were also going to have a
hot chocolate table, and they are planning to
donate all proceeds to charity."

Welp. Clem gulped. "Oh, I didn't realize.
Well, I don't have to offer hot—"

"No, no. I wasn't saying that to deter you
from serving, I just thought you should
know."

"Really, it's okay. I don't want to compete
with them if they are doing it for a cause, you

know? I don't mind giving them that. I can just do coffee and if people want hot chocolates, I'll send them to the Scouts?"

Polly smiled, clearly going back into her event organizing brain space. "I will let them know".

I'm sure you will... Clementine thought. "All right, I'll let you get to it, it looks like others are waiting for your attention," she said, nodding towards Joe, who was standing with the restaurant owner, Brent, deep in conversation, though it appeared that Joe wasn't listening to anything Brent was saying and was staring at the girls instead.

Polly shooed her hand and rolled her eyes. "I'm sure Joe wants to discuss the new mural they are planning for the side of this building."

Clementine nodded. "Take care." She turned as Polly said her goodbyes and headed toward Joe and Brent. She didn't want to get caught by anyone else. She certainly didn't want to get caught by Brent. She couldn't look at anyone in that room without scrutinizing their motives, where they were, or if they knew anything about the case. She didn't know where to go from here, apart from heading back to her roastery and trying to get her feet grounded again, in any way she could.

Though, if she was certain about one thing, it was this: Paul Wright did not die by suicide. Paul Wright was murdered. And there was a great possibility that the killer... was sitting inside this community hall.

CHAPTER
FIVE

The cobblestone sidewalk protruded under the thin soles of her shoes as she crossed the road, chucking her coffee cup in a nearby trash can. She was free. Nobody followed her out of the meeting hall to chat afterwards. Her mental capacity for socializing had been maxed out, and the idea of getting back to what she loved was just in sight: feeling the green beans in her hands as she weighed them out, smelling what else had grown in the soil with them, and thinking about the farmers and how they produced these beans. She had the opportunity to work with them and showcase their flavor profiles in the best way possible. The roasting facility meant getting away from the gossip and the people and the scrutinizing and the questions and the judgment and the fate of her future— away from it all.

She approached the building, hopped up on the curb, and headed for the door when something yellow flapped in the wind and caught her attention. It made her halt and narrow her eyes. When she noticed what it was, her spine straightened and a tightness gripped her throat. A bit of crime scene tape must have broken off and got caught on some foliage. She hadn't thought she'd be this affected coming back to the roastery after her break. This place was her haven. She had felt productive, calm, and safe here. She hadn't even entered the building yet, and she was overcome with vulnerability, nausea, and … *fear*.

Clementine folded her arms and gave herself a hug, rubbing her hands down her tattooed biceps. She shook her head and turned away from the facility, looking at the surrounding buildings before heading back to her car.

Once inside, she slammed the door shut and locked the car, putting her head in her hands in exasperation. She wanted to scream out her frustration, but she just sat there a moment in the silence of the car, muffled from the sounds of the outside cars passing. Clementine leaned over in her seat and reached for her cell phone. She pulled up her contacts.

Perhaps she just needed support. To not be alone. To be with someone, like a buddy system, not just with Robusta. Ro made good company, but she couldn't call for help if help was needed.

So Clementine sat in the car and grappled with going into the building, or staying frozen right where she was. Surely nothing would happen now, in broad daylight, lots of witnesses in the neighboring businesses and on the street. Everyone was mostly on high alert. And even if she didn't believe that Paul had died by suicide, perhaps it was an isolated, targeted incident. Perhaps someone just had it out for Paul specifically, and that had nothing to do with her. And that was half a month ago, with no news or updates since. Maybe she just needed backup.

She could call the shop, but she assumed that Josie and the rest of the team were busy with a catering group this morning along with their regular traffic. None of them would be able to break away to come help her.

She looked back down at her phone and sighed. "Okay… I'm doin' it," she called out into the silence. She pulled up Simon's contact. He did say she could reach out whenever she needed something. Perhaps she was being overly paranoid. Perhaps she would make herself look weak. Perhaps he would enjoy feeling needed. Or maybe he would think she was making a pass at him. At any rate, she needed to work. Her place of work now gave her anxiety and made her feel unsafe. And her new acquaintance was a cop who was in tune with the case… which could also be in her investigative interest, especially after the information she'd just learned at the community meeting. She *did* want to get to the bottom of what the captain said and perhaps Simon could give her some insight.

"All right. Enough talking myself into this." She dialed the number.

"Officer Drake speaking."

Her throat went dry. How official. How intimidating. Of course he wouldn't recognize her number, because he was the one that put his number into her phone. He'd only have her number if she'd reciprocated it. She hadn't until now. Perhaps he was thinking she would have reached out that same night. But it'd been an entire couple of weeks. By now he'd probably completely forgotten about her or thought she'd blown him off.

"Hi—" She cleared her throat. She hated talking on the phone. This was awkward. She should have texted. *Oh my.* Why did she call?

"Clem?"

He got to it before she could even respond. That made her lip turn up into a small smile, calming her panicked breathing. "Yes, hi, Officer."

"I told you to call me Simon. What's going on? Are you okay?" His tone was pointed. Serious.

"I'm okay," she said "I mean… I think? I'm at the roasting building for the first time since… well you know. And I can't bring myself to go inside. Is that… dumb?"

There was quiet on the line for a moment. "That's absolutely not dumb. Are you alone?" he asked.

"Mm hm. I usually am when I'm over here. I didn't know it would be as hard as it is, but I need to get some work done."

"I'm on my way."

"… well, I mean, I don't want to interrupt you if you're busy doing something." She stifled a small laugh.

"I'm doing radar down the road, Clem. I can be at your place in a few minutes."

She reached up to her lips, unable to stop them from smiling more widely. Though she liked his insistence, an immediate pang of guilt emerged. "Well I mean, I appreciate it. But it's no big deal. I shouldn't have called. I'll just, uhh, I'll be okay." She started backpedaling.

"I'm coming. Stay where you are." The line cut. He'd hung up.

"Oh man." She sighed into the car, looking around at her surroundings before putting the phone in her lap. If anything, she may have saved a few drivers from a speeding ticket.

It didn't take long for the police cruiser to pull into the lot of the roasting facility. When Clementine saw it in her rearview mirror, she relaxed. Which was quite funny, because prior to knowing Simon, she'd never felt that emotion when she saw a police car in her rearview. She'd gotten a couple of tickets in her life, and generally cops had a reputation for being no-nonsense. She'd always panic because of the cost of paying the ticket, and even more money was required to hire a lawyer to clear the ticket, something that she'd only had the privilege of doing once.

Clementine grabbed her bag, keys, and phone and got out of the car. She stopped a moment, then hit the remote on her key fob to lock it. Never before did she think to lock her car in Roastwood Hollow. But now, she wasn't so sure. She pushed her orange locks over her shoulders and looked up at Simon, her cheeks warming. She reached up and touched them, looking at him as she approached.

"Hey, it's no worries. We'll make sure it's clear, okay?" He pulled a flashlight from his belt, held it up by his chin, and clicked it on.

She nodded. He knew what to say before

she could even open her mouth. Had the embarrassment been plastered across her forehead? She led the way to the side door and put her key in the lock, opening it. She looked over her shoulder at him.

"You want me to go in first?" he asked.

She did. But she already looked like a wimp, and wasn't usually this vulnerable, and didn't like the way it felt, so she shook her head. "I can go. Just come with me."

"Right behind ya."

She flipped the light switch and walked into the facility, Simon's footsteps sounded behind her. Everything was exactly the way she'd left it, with a few things askew, most likely from the investigators who were in the building after she'd left. After setting her bag and keys down on the prep table, she walked straight over to where her stock of roasted beans sat.

"I'm going to check the back." Simon said quietly, gesturing towards the utility room. The room where it all happened.

She nodded and turned back to the beans. She lifted up the lid to an Ethiopian roast, the aroma wafting out to hit her in the face. This coffee had been sitting on the shelf a week since it'd been roasted, which was typically longer than she liked to get it out. Though, because it was left whole bean, it would still be a delicious and fresh cup. She counted the rest of what she had on the shelves and took stock of how many batches and which country origins she'd need to roast for this session. All the while, she kept her ear open for Simon to return, which he did momentarily.

"It's all clear, Clem. Nothing is amiss, doors locked. Everything has been cleaned up by the CSI crew. The bleach smell has evaporated. But I will stay with you. You shouldn't be here alone anyway." He scratched the back of his head as he looked around the large warehouse space.

She nodded and gave him a small smile. "I really appreciate it, Officer."

"I told you to call me Simon." He smiled. "It's weird when you call me Officer Drake, okay? I appreciate the respect, but I'm here as a friend."

She nodded. "Do you... want some coffee?" It was only natural. She wanted to do what she did best to get back in the groove. Plus, she did want to quality control the beans on the shelf to make sure they were still up to par.

"Of course," he answered. "Is there anything I can do to help?"

"No, you can just hang out. I have chairs over there." She pointed to her makeshift breakroom: two comfy chairs with a milk crate wrapped in a burlap sack as the coffee table between them. "Robusta's favorite spot is in that window."

He headed that way, and Clementine went to her mini kitchenette that held all the supplies she needed to brew a coffee. Usually she would do something called a cupping to test quality control, because it stripped all the variables from affecting the aroma and flavor of the coffee, but cupping was a whole ceremony. This time, it made more sense to stick with a single cup brewing process, like a pour-over. She pulled a ceramic cone from the cupboard along with a mug. Inching the scale close to the edge of the counter to start the process, it was like a familiar walk in the park. Measure the beans. Grind them. Heat the water.

A chill danced across her shoulders and the back of her neck, a sudden awareness of Simon's gaze on her. She lifted the electric kettle from its base. The thermometer read that it was just above boiling. Water flowed from the metal gooseneck of the kettle and rinsed the paper filter inside the cone-shaped vessel. Clem tossed out the water that dripped into the mug, then tapped her finger on the back of the paper cup that held the coffee grounds and watched them tumble into the filter.

"Why do you do that?"

She stole a quick glance over her shoulder at him. "What, wet the filter?"

"Mm hmm."

"For a few reasons." She went back to her work, pouring with precision from the kettle, wetting over the grounds in a single layer, then backing it off and putting a timer on for thirty seconds. "To get rid of the paper taste of the filter, and to preheat the cone before brewing." The concentration on the task made her feel at home. Comfort. Familiarity. The attention from Simon didn't even bother her. Being a barista for many years before she moved into roasting had trained her to have watchful eyes on her work. It used to make her nervous, as though customers were scrutinizing what she was doing. However, with experience comes the realization that they were mostly genuinely curious about the process, rather than waiting for her to mess it up.

Clementine turned the timer off at twenty-eight seconds, then continued to pour the water from the kettle onto the coffee grounds in a circular motion until the water reached the top of the cone. The grounds bloomed, puffing up with a single bubble of air emerging near the center, almost as though the coffee itself was breathing life, something coffee grounds did during the brewing process when they were fresh. Before even tasting the coffee, Clem concluded that it would pass her quality control check. Didn't matter that the coffee was a week old, it was still fresher than you could get in most places.

As the coffee deflated in the cone, it dripped out the bottom side into the mug below. The aroma was sweet, with hints of nutty goodness. She did another sweep with the kettle in a circular motion up to the top of the cone, then set it down on the table with ease.

She spun around toward the sitting area and leaned with both palms on the stainless steel prep table. "Nearly there," she said quietly. "Simon?" Suddenly her throat constricted, the breath escaping her lungs. Her palms went clammy, and she moved them from the table before they slid off from the sweat and she embarrassed herself.

"Yeah?" He moved to the edge of the chair at attention.

"I wanted to ask you about… you know." She glanced over to the back room and then back to him.

"Ahh" He shook his head and backed up on the chair. "Now you know I can't share anything about the case with you, Clem." It was a matter of fact.

She stared a moment with her piercing green eyes, pushing a piece of her fiery orange hair behind her ear. "I just want to know that it isn't closed," she said, straight to the point.

"Why are you asking this?" A crease formed between his eyes, a mark of concern.

"At the community meeting earlier... Captain said that they deemed Paul's death a suicide. I just don't see that as true." She stared into him, to catch any signs or clues from his body language.

A silence loomed between them. "Did you only ask me here to get information out of me on the case? Here I thought you... I thought..." He stood and paced a moment, then looked up at her.

Her chest tightened. He thought what? She didn't want to give him the chance to finish that. "I asked you here because I didn't feel safe coming in here. You told me to call you if I needed anything. I thought you were someone I could call on if I didn't feel safe." She straightened her lips and stared, point blank.

He nodded. "You can."

"Then what's the problem?"

He sighed, a bit of growl in it. "Listen. The autopsy showed... evidence that his death may have been self-inflicted. They found a substance..." He paused. "Clem, I could lose my job."

The way he raised his eyebrow gave her a

flutter in her stomach. She pushed that feeling down, way down. "I won't tell anyone, I swear."

"They found a substance that predated the knife injury. They think the knife was inflicted to make it staged that it was someone else. But the substance is ultimately what did it. And nobody else had a key to the building... well except you."

She crossed her arms. The tattooed yellow, orange, and red flowers across her biceps and forearms were stark against the black sleeve-less tank. "I was already in here." She narrowed her eyes. "And I have an alibi."

He laughed. "Do you think I'd be hanging out with you here alone if I thought you were a murderer?"

"Maybe. You could be tailing me to see if I slip up." She shrugged, then looked over her shoulder at the grounds in the cone. The water was still draining from them.

"Are you going to?" he asked, serious and straight-faced, though the energy was still light and playful.

This was banter, but it was a distraction. He wasn't telling her what she wanted to hear. "Of course not. Because I didn't do it. But I can tell you, somebody else did. Paul would never—"

"Clem. You need to drop this. Please. Do

you think forensics would just let this go if they had found evidence that pointed in that direction? This case is being put to rest. The family needs peace, they need answers."

"Yeah, but the wrong answers—"

"Clementine."

She pursed her lips. She could tell his frustration had matched hers. He crossed the room towards her. She tensed, gripping her arms tighter. The presence of him in his uniform was so strong. Most of the time, people shied away from her because of her look. But he didn't. He didn't treat her like she was a punk, or a criminal. He stood right in front of her. "Promise me you will drop this, okay? It's for your own good."

"What is that supposed to mean?" she asked, not allowing her intimidation to show.

"It means, I don't want you poking around in this any further."

"Well, that makes me think you are hiding something." She turned her back to him. He towered over her in height. She took the pour-over off the mug, disposed of the filter and grounds, then picked up the coffee mug and turned around, pushing it into his chest.

"I'm not. I just don't want you getting in trouble. Or obsessing over something that's been put to bed."

She shook her head slightly, disagreeing

with him once more, but saw where this was going. Simon was on the side of the police, the side of the captain, the side where they said this whole thing was death by suicide and they wouldn't investigate it any further.

"What if…"

He took the mug from her and sighed.

"No, hear me out. I can't help but think that if, and only if, you guys are wrong, then there is an actual madman killer out there."

Simon put his free hand on the side of her arm. "I will not let anyone hurt you."

She blushed, unable to help it. "I appreciate that… enjoy the coffee." She turned away from him and fussed with the materials on the counter.

Simon walked back towards the chairs, sipping the mug. "Oh wow, that is… dang that is far better than what they serve at the station."

She chuckled under her breath. "Thank you."

Clem wished she knew Simon well enough to ask him if he was telling her to back off because he was in training. As a new cop, she respected that he needed to play by the rules and stay in line when he was just getting his footing. The notorious police-in-training in this town never let anyone off without a ticket. Not even the previous town mayor, who tried to get out of a ticket by calling the chief on her cell phone while the new cop was at her car window writing it down.

The point was, he didn't want her to poke into this case, that much was clear. Regardless of the information he'd given her about the autopsy report, she didn't trust the results. She was going to have to be sly about this. All she had to do was what everyone in this town already did—talk to each other. Weed out what information was useful to her and what information was simply just gossip.

Clem walked over to the roaster and ran her hand along it, rounding the cooling bin to the control panel on the side. She hovered over the first toggle a moment, images of the last time she'd touched this machine flashing in her mind. She had to overcome it.

She flipped on the drum motor first. The roaster hummed to life. Then the blower. Then the gas and ignitor. The burners underneath the drum glowed blue with the hottest flame, and then caught onto the rest of the burners. She looked at the thermometer to confirm it was trending upwards, then turned to Simon, who was looking at his phone, that same brow furrowed.

"Hey, you can go if you need to," she called out, her voice louder over the sound of the roaster. One of the reasons why she hadn't heard any commotion in the back room the day that Paul was found. The machine was so loud.

Simon stood again. "You sure? I mean, I can stay."

"I know you're busy. And this is just going to be boring at this point. You've proven that I'm in here alone and everything is secure, yeah?"

He nodded. "Yeah. I mean, I do need to get back to my post. But listen, I'm not far, okay? I can come back at any time. If you're in here roasting and get spooked, please just text. Okay?"

She nodded. "I appreciate that."

He held up the mug of steaming coffee as though he was toasting to her. "Ima keep this," he slurred.

That got a small laugh from her. " 'Kay, but you'll need to give me that mug back when you're done. They're limited here."

"Gives me another reason to see you."

Or to keep his eye on me, she thought. She needed to be careful, because the person who could give her insight had also told her to back off. He just didn't know her well enough yet. because she was not going to let up on figuring out who had killed Paul.

The killer was still out there.

CHAPTER
SIX

Only a few completed batches decorated the shelves before Clementine's phone vibrated in her pocket with a text from Josie. A woman was over at the coffeehouse asking for her. At first Clem thought it was probably a sales call, but Josie was pretty good at differentiating between something real and a cold call; warding off those who weren't important. She texted back that it would be a few minutes and asked if they would wait for her to finish up, whoever it was.

She guided the roasted beans out of the cooling bin and into the storage container, weighed the bin, and then marked down the humidity loss on her chart. Next came labeling the bin, lidding it, and placing it on the shelf with the others. While waiting for the roaster to cool down, she cleaned up the

roasting area, swept fallen beans, and organized labels and papers on the prep tables.
The roaster needed to completely cool.
Turning off a four hundred degree machine
without dropping its heat was a good way to
warp the drum, which was the last thing she
wanted.

When it was at a low enough temperature,
Clementine powered the roaster down and
hung up her denim apron. She pulled her
wavy, red hair up into a messy bun on the top
of her head, revealing a few more delicate tattoos on the small of her back and shoulders.
Then she threw on a black zipper hoodie and
left the facility, making sure to lock it
behind her.

A chill loomed in the air and she zipped
up the hoodie as she reached the shop. The
bell on the door dinged as she entered. The
aroma of the coffee she'd roasted wafted
under her nose as it brewed behind the
counter, alongside the smell of cinnamon
sweetness; something was always baking in
the kitchen. The fruits of her labor were fully
ripened in this building. Though she didn't
work here much anymore, unless they were
absolutely desperate for someone to cover a
shift, it was nice to see where all her hard
work was enjoyed. She spent a lot of time in
the roastery by herself, which is why she

would often bring Robusta, since the roastery wasn't customer-facing. She walked through the cafe to the counter, catching Josie's attention.

"Hey! Soo... the lady in the back window booth seat. Says she's part of the Wright estate. I figured that you'd want to take this meeting."

Clementine's heart panged. "Yes, thank you. Definitely." Her green eyes pierced the back of the shop, spotting the woman in the pantsuit. She made a b-line for the booth, then cleared her throat.

"Hello? Hi, I'm Clementine Matthews." She put out her hand for the woman to shake.

The woman with the pantsuit and blond bob haircut reached out and shook her hand, gesturing to the seat across from her. "Hi there, yes. I was hoping to catch you here. I'm the executor representing the Wright family and their estate."

Clem looked back and forth and then slipped into the booth, just as a business card was pushed across the table toward her. *Annette Rhoads, Legal Personal Representative.*

"I understand you are the tenant of the building on Oak Street?"

Clementine's breathing quickened as though her lungs shrunk. She wiped her clammy hands on her jeans under the table.

This could be it. The answer she'd been waiting to hear. This meeting could change the course of everything in her future. Was she going to have to move her entire roasting business? What was the fate of that building?

"Yes. Yeah, I rent that space for my roastery," she responded quietly.

"Okay, well the family has decided to sell…"

Clementine froze. The walls started to close in around her vision. She tried not to freak out inside. The lady wasn't finished explaining. Maybe there was more to it.

"…but they have explained a few options here for you."

It was then Clem noticed the manila folder on the table between them. and the woman shuffling papers into different stacks, as if looking for something.

Options. Options were good. This could be good.

"Upon the sale of the building, you as the tenant would have first right of refusal to whoever decides to bid. But before that, they want to extend the offer to you to buy it. Whether you buy it outright, or if you want to engage in a rent-to-own agreement."

This was a lot of information. It seemed to make sense, but it was all so overwhelming. At this point, the lady was done talking and staring at her. A bit of mascara had flaked off the woman's eyelashes and lay on her cheekbone. Clementine couldn't help but stare at that small fleck.

"Ms. Matthews?"

She heard the woman speak as though she were at the end of a tunnel.

"If you need time to think about this, the family will understand. But we do need to come to a decision and move quickly, so they can plan for putting the building on the market…if it comes to that."

Clem heard that statement plain as day. "Yeah," she spoke out, her voice cracked. "I'm sorry. Yes. I hear what you are saying. Everything is just happening so quickly. I'm still not used to the fact that Paul is gone."

The woman nodded, looking down at her paperwork and then back at Clem. She had empathy in her eyes. She'd been working with the family. Clem guessed she'd gotten her fair share of grief from the clients. This was probably one of her easy meetings.

And Clem was acting crazy, so she felt. "I am interested, of course. I need to, uhh… contact a few of my resources before I make a final decision on which way to go though. But I can do this with urgency, if that's what's required." Clem was proud of how she responded. She was elated to have the options in the first place. It didn't appear that they were interested in uprooting her, or taking everything away, in spite of the recent tragedy they had endured.

"Of course, take the time you need. We'll likely need a response in about seventy-two hours, but if you need anything from me in the meantime, you now have my card."

Clementine scooped it up. She was reeling at the possibilities in front of her, though wasn't sure how it could work. She was broke. She needed to get in touch with the bank and see about a loan. That was a good place to start. There was always the possibility of investors, but she didn't want to complicate things further by adding more people to the picture, or owing anyone, or needing to pay people back. Crowdfunding was available, but she was never one to straight up ask for money either. She liked to be independent and get things on her own: work for them. That was how it had always been.

"Ms. Rhoads?" she called, reading the name off the business card in her hand. "I just have to ask before I go…" She looked up at the lady, who was putting down her latte mug after taking a sip.

"Why did Mrs. Wright choose to work with me on this, instead of just getting rid of the building?" She wasn't sure if she'd get an answer. Or if Annette Rhoads even knew. But if she didn't ask, then it would bother her until she got something.

"Well, for one, Paul Wright owned many buildings, and she isn't offering this same deal to some of the other tenants, if that tells you anything about her regard for you specifically."

Clem's heart panged. That was just so genuinely nice. She had always been on time with her rent. And Paul and his family frequented Josie's coffee shop. He was still a landlord, and landlords got a bad reputation for being... well, landlordly. But she did genuinely feel a misting in her eyes at the sentiment.

"Not only that. Mrs. Wright told me that everything was taken from her, but she didn't want the same to happen to you and your business."

Clem nodded, her eyes welling. She choked tears back. She wasn't going to cry in front of this executor. "Well that is much, much appreciated, I hope she knows that." Her voice wavered, and she cleared her throat. "I will get back to you—" Clem tapped the business card on the table, "—within the next couple of days after I've straightened some things out. Thank you for stopping in, and for waiting for me to get here." She stood and put the woman's business card in her back pocket. This was all business, but it really was a class act on Paul's family's part to consider her situation before selling the building.

Though, she wasn't out of the woods just yet. The consideration was there, but she still had to pull through and make it happen. Of course, if she couldn't purchase the building, then there was the rent-to-own option, it would just be a longer process.

All of these thoughts rushed into her as she walked back up to the front counter, making eye contact with Josie.

"You need a cold brew?" she asked Clem, drying her hands on a paper towel.

She smiled. "I need something a little stronger than that," she said under her breath. "Thanks for telling me I had this appointment. It was definitely important."

"Chat with me about it later, 'kay?" Josie scooted over to the espresso machine and back into the swing of making the drinks on the counter.

"Yeah." Clem agreed, "later." She nodded in goodbye, and then took off through the front door, a rush of cool winter air welcoming her into the Roastwood Hollow streets.

CHAPTER
SEVEN

T he next morning, Clementine smoothed her hands over her denim romper and adjusted the black cardigan over her shoulders. She covered up her tattoos for the meeting at the bank, even though most of the tellers and personal bankers knew her in this small town where everyone knew everyone. Those in the coffee industry got some leeway when it came to personal expression versus professionalism. The generations above her tended to associate tattoos with unprofessionalism. She'd heard that enough from her parents.

She pulled her bag in front of her body and peeked inside inconspicuously. Robusta poked her little head up and blinked at Clementine. Clem petted her scaly head and pushed her back into the bag with care.

Surely this was the first time a bearded

dragon was ever inside a banking institution. She would have Robusta with her at the roastery all day today. A new confidence washed over her after her meeting with the executor of the Wright's estate. She moved up in line towards the bank teller, tucking her bag closer to her. Robusta was generally good at staying hidden while in public places. Of course the reptile liked the harness and leash better—more room for exploring—but Clem knew the little beardy liked being close to her as well.

Clementine looked around the bank. She hadn't been there in a while. Not since she last took deposits here for the coffeehouse, when she still worked with Josie. It was a gorgeous setup, the building restored to its appearance before the town had flooded several decades ago. They'd replaced all the old tile and light fixtures, as well as some old-timey teller stands and functional decor. It was fascinating to see the aesthetic and think about what it must have looked like in its prime. Very elegant. The coffeehouse often gave off a vibe like that. The buildings in Roastwood Hollow's downtown were very old, and with that came lots of old problems, but she loved the vintage flair as opposed to the many modern coffee shops that the third-wave specialty coffee movement brought. Subway tiles.

Marble counters. Straight lines. Not Roastwood.

"Hi Clem," the teller called her forward.

She approached the counter. "Hi Sandy. Can I please speak with one of the personal bankers?" She nodded to the office. "I have some financial profile questions." She rocked on her feet, looking sideways at her surroundings.

"Of course, go ahead and have a seat and I will get one of them." Sandy was sweet, and she sure put up with a lot. Clem nodded and walked over to a small sitting area. A fake Christmas tree stood in the corner by the sitting area, decorated in red and gold, with present boxes underneath. It was still only early November, but this town was decorated early. It reminded her of the discussions about the Snowflake Festival at the meeting yesterday morning, which seemed like forever ago. Had that really only been yesterday that she sat frustrated at that community meeting, listening to them drone on about a festival, when there were more important things at hand? More people stood behind her in line, but she kept her head down and sat on the hunter green armchair, recoiling to herself. She didn't want to get into any conversations right then, and besides, it seemed that some of the townspeople were still avoiding her. Josie informed her that she'd heard whispers in the coffeehouse about how they didn't want to trigger her, since Clem was there the night Paul was found. If that was the case, she almost welcomed that. Let them think they might trigger her. She didn't want to talk to them anyway.

"Clementine? Hey, come on in." Greg said, standing in the doorframe of his office, wearing a navy blue banking suit. He was her dad's age, and when it came to business and banking, his stereotype dominated the industry. She didn't care much about that, as long as she was able to borrow the money she needed. This was going to be interesting, especially with Robusta in her purse. But it was worth a shot. She stood up quickly and followed Greg into his office, closing the door behind her.

The glass walls in his office lent no privacy visually, which was both good and bad. Anyone could see that she was in there talking to the personal banker, but they couldn't hear what she was saying. And people were going to talk, regardless. She was certain that Peggy across the street at the old insurance agent's office had seen her walk into the bank. And if she'd taken longer than the time it takes to make a normal deposit while being in there, she must be up to something.

"So, what brings you in here today? How's the coffee coming along?"

"Uh yeah, it's great. Busy." She shuffled in the chair. "As I'm sure you already know, the building that houses my roastery is changing ownership. I'm here to see if I could qualify to purchase the building from Paul's family. And I should have said this at the beginning, but I'd appreciate it if we could keep this between us." She looked over her shoulder and then back.

"Of course. Everything we discuss about any of your accounts is confidential, Clementine. Why would it not be?"

She gave him a skeptical look. "I know you are likely to talk with Sandy if questions come up. And Sandy can't... keep *anything* confidential, you know that. And this is such a hot topic right now. I know this won't be kept secret for long, but right now I just don't know what direction it's going to go, and I'd rather not be public with it quite yet."

"Of course, of course. Let me pull some numbers here." He clicked on his keyboard, "Is that... a lizard?" He paused his typing and reached across his desk for his readers, perching them on the tip of his nose.

Clem shifted again, then pulled her bag closer. "Oops, sorry. It's my beardy, Robusta."

"We've never had…a *beardy* in the bank before." His voice was higher pitched and uncertain.

She smirked. "Yeah, a bearded dragon. Sorry, she's my pet. I have to have her with me today. I didn't think we'd be here long. She won't disturb anything."

He laughed. "I'll tell ya, it's never boring in this town, is it?"

That was just something people said. But she couldn't help but feel a tightness in her throat. Never boring? Someone dying is for your entertainment?

Greg wasn't like that. But one more community meeting, and she may convince herself that the people in this town thrived on the hardship of others.

The clicking resumed from Greg's keyboard and brought her back to reality.

Robusta *was* being good; she stuck her little spiky head out of the purse and rested it on the side. Clem had her in a crocheted orange sweater today. Usually she just took a sock and cut holes for her bearded dragon to wear, but today she decided to dress her in the little sweater she had bought at a local craft fair.

"It looks like we can definitely put in an

application. All your information looks good on this end. It'll depend on how much you need to source, and if we do a seven or ten year…" He clicked on the keyboard some more. "Bottom line, Clementine, is…" He pulled his eyes away from the computer and adjusted his keyboard, then focused on her.

Her stomach flipped. It was like he held the fate of her future in his hands. She was hopeful but didn't even know where she stood.

"…we could make this work with collateral or a guarantor. And you could use your equipment for collateral. So I say you have a pretty good shot at weighing your options between direct purchase or rent to own. This is hopeful."

"Yes, very," she confirmed, trying to contain her excitement. "Thanks so much, Greg. If you want to go ahead and submit that, I can go back to the executor and let them know I can move forward in some capacity at least."

He smiled, folding his hands on the desk. "I'm glad I could help out. It pays to use a small-town bank over one of the big guys who just treat you like a number. We want to keep our dollars in our community, and we want you to succeed with Roastwood Coffee."

"Well, I appreciate that." She stood, pushing back the chair. "We'll be in touch?"

Greg matched her standing. "Absolutely."

She nodded, unable to hide her relieved smile, and headed for the door.

"If I need you to sign anything, I'll email it over, okay?"

"Thank you!" The lift in her mood gave her confidence. It'd been quite a stressful week, and she would take the small wins when she could.

She left the office. The whole bank was a blur as she walked past the glistening gold of the Christmas tree on her way to the entrance, when a large shadow loomed in front of the light coming through the glass door. Someone was coming toward her. She moved over to allow the person to pass by her in the tight space, but this person was not passing by, they were headed right at her. She refocused her attention. It was the restaurant owner from across the street.

She didn't usually pay much attention to him. In fact, she'd tended to purposefully avoid him, because of things she'd heard over the years from the baristas at the shop. One time, one of the young baristas was in need of a second job. She interviewed over at The Diner, and the owner, Brent, glossed over all the questions with her. She specifically said that he leaned across the desk and said to her in an ominous tone, "You could make me a *lot* of money," referring to her behind the bar. And he was *not* talking about her bartending skills. It was weird. Ick. Clementine always let that guide her view of the man and she just sort of stayed clear. Not to mention, he was a big bad businessman, the epitome of one. It was hard to find anything in common with him. She'd be cordial, of course, especially at the community meetings and such, but that was the extent of it.

"Hey there." His voice was booming, commanding.

Clem looked everywhere but at him as he backed her into the space between the Christmas tree and the wall. He was blocking her only path to the door, and she couldn't go around him even if she wanted to. He towered over her.

"Hi, I need to get going so if you'll excuse me." She advanced, but he didn't budge. His lips parted into a smile surrounded by a halo goatee. She furrowed her brow. Was he really not going to let her pass?

"I heard a rumor that you were going to buy the building your roastery is in."

What? She'd *just* left the office. Surely the news didn't travel *that* fast? He couldn't have known. Perhaps he eavesdropped, or someone else eavesdropped at the coffee-house when she talked with Annette Rhoads.

Or… or it could all just be speculation at this point.

"Sorry, I don't know what you're talking about. Just a rumor." She shrugged, training her eyes on him with a very serious look. Her heart actually raced. She didn't like being cornered or made to feel vulnerable. Was *nobody* else seeing this in the bank? It was as if time slowed.

"Listen. I make a lot of money with my two diners. I run two half a billion dollar businesses. I'll buy that building, and you run your business in it."

The nerve. He had *no* clue what her financial situation was. And she sure as heck wasn't going to brag about it. He had to be bluffing. There's no way he had this information. She smiled sweetly, trying to defuse the situation.

She had to get out.

Needed to get out.

She couldn't allow him to feel this power over her. "I don't know what you're talking about." She half-smiled. "But uhh, thanks for the offer. Good luck." She moved to push past him, but he still didn't move.

Then he jumped back, a look of disgust on his face. "What the…"

At first she thought he was intimidated by her commanding attempt push past him, and then her purse jostled. Robusta had made an appearance yet again. This time, the underside of her head, her beard, had darkened in color. This was a sure sign she was stressed. Robusta vibrated, puffing out her spiky back.

"Clementine!"

She heard her name over to the side, and took the opportunity to escape. If not for herself, for the sake of her stressed bearded dragon. "Yeah?" She took a moment to make eye contact one last time with Brent, then broke her gaze to focus on the voice who'd just interrupted them.

Greg was leaning in his doorframe. "I forgot, there actually was something I needed your signature on."

She glanced back at Brent and then back to Greg. She turned, escaping his big shadow and tucking Robusta back in her bag. What was he getting at? Did he really think he could intimidate her? She would never go into business with him, even in the most desperate of situations. She'd rather go bankrupt than work with him or for him, that was for sure.

Clem rushed by the large man and headed for Greg's office. She stole a quick glance over her shoulder. He'd already gone up to the teller window to conduct whatever other business he had.

"I can sign it real quick."

"Yeah, there's nothing to sign. I just saw you getting cornered by Brent and thought you could use some assistance."

She heaved a big exhale. "Wow. Okay. Uh, yeah. Thank you. You're the real MVP, Greg. I seriously appreciate you."

He laughed. "Of course. I'm sure you and that … thing…"

"It's a bearded dragon," she laughed.

"Yes, that. I'm sure you could have figured it out, but I really can't stand that guy."

She sobered, nodding. "Is he gone?"

He nodded. "Just left. Take it easy, ok?"

Her shoulders slumped, relaxed. "Thank you, Greg."

She had learned a lot at the bank today. It had been very productive. She learned that it was possible for her to purchase the building her roastery was in, whether it was immediate or took longer to achieve. She also learned that Brent had moved up to the top of her suspect list.

Why did he want that building so badly? And would he do anything he could to get what he wanted… including murder?

CHAPTER
EIGHT

"Are you sure this isn't a date?" Josie asked as they rounded the corner and headed for The Diner.

"No. Of course it's not."

"But he was the one who asked you if you wanted to get a bite to eat."

Clementine laughed and watched her footing on the cobblestone sidewalk. "Listen. Simon and I are just getting to know each other. It was weird how we met, but he's new to the town, and I'm still trying to get back in the swing of things after... you know. Plus, I haven't eaten at The Diner in a while and I like to support local, support our town."

Josie's eyes glossed over. "You hate Brent."

Clem stifled a small laugh. "What? What do you mean?"

"You only always complain about him."

"You're not wrong... but The Diner is convenient, you know?"

They made it to the door and Clementine reached for the handle, ushering Josie inside first and following behind them.

Of course Josie was right. Clem did hate Brent. She complained about him all the time: his business antics, his egotistical behavior. But after the incident in the bank earlier that day, which she hadn't told anyone about, she wanted to keep an eye on him and gather more information. And this was all against the advice of Simon, who had told her to back off.

They snuck past the small crowd of patrons gathered in the lobby and she spotted Simon sitting at one of the round back tables. He stood when they entered the room and waved them over. He wasn't in his police uniform, but a regular hunter green t-shirt and jeans. She'd not see him yet off duty, and it really threw her off. She smiled as they made their way over.

"Hi?" He looked from Clem to Josie and back to Clem.

"Josie." She reached forward and shook hands with Simon, her curly shoulder length hair bouncing as they moved aside. "We met briefly that night at the ... roastery. I took Robusta home for Clem."

Simon closed his momentarily gaping

mouth and nodded, recollection surfacing on his expression. "Oh yeah, I remember. I'm Simon."

Josie leaned into Clementine. "He did NOT know I was going to be here. Seriously?"

Clementine smiled and pushed her off, pulling out the chair on Simon's other side as they both sat.

"Hi," he said quickly to Clem, training his eyes back on the menu as he sat.

Clem turned to Josie. "When I suggested we come to The Diner, Simon asked me, 'Which diner?' And I said, '*The* Diner.' " They both laughed.

"Who knew the name of the diner was The Diner." He shrugged.

"All of Roastwood Hollow." Josie laughed.

Simon cleared his throat. "Good day, then?" he asked quickly, flipping the menu over.

"Yeah, it was okay." Clem glanced down quickly at the menu in front of her. She felt a little guilty tagging Josie along. But Simon didn't specify that this was a date exactly. She had way too much going on to focus on dating, especially now. Simon was nice enough, and she was getting to know him more lately, given the circumstances, but why would she want to get close to someone romantically that she knew wasn't going to be around long?

He'd already told her that he was likely to be transferred to a different precinct once his field training was complete.

Though, also given the circumstances, she was comforted by his presence. She was safe when he was around. And these days, that was a place she craved.

A waitress came and set down waters, letting them know she'd be back momentarily for their orders.

"Do you think they have anything vegan here?" Josie asked.

Clementine nearly spit-taked on the table after taking a sip of water from the thick plastic textured cup. "I highly doubt it. I'm sure there's a salad or something, but it's probably doused in some kind of dairy-based dressing. You could always ask though." She felt Simon's gaze on her, so she looked over her menu at him. The look he gave her was longing, and she shrugged, trying to look apologetic. Though, she didn't owe him anything. And he hadn't been specific. They were just hanging out. And she had spy work to do.

"You should try the chicken fried steak." She pointed out to Simon, and then wandered her gaze over to the bar, and the door that led to the kitchens. Surely Brent was around somewhere, and if he wasn't, then she may be able to get one of his employees chatting.

Brent's office was actually in the building behind the restaurant; she'd passed it many times walking through the town. Perhaps she'd come up with a reason to go there, though she wasn't sure she'd find any 'evidence' in there anyhow. It crossed her mind that if she was going to get into this spy stuff, maybe she could plant a recording device there. She took another sip of water and rubbed the back of her neck.

"Hey, I'm going to go to the bathroom, but could you order me the beef au jus sandwich?" she asked, directing the question at Josie. She looked at Simon and mouthed, 'I'll be right back', and then turned and headed for the bathroom.

In the single bathroom, she stared at herself in the mirror, hands dangling by her sides. She knew exactly what she was doing, bringing Josie along. She was trying to provide a distraction so that she could collect information on the case. Why she hadn't just come on her own without Simon, or clarified his intentions, was a different mystery.

She was just getting to know him. It felt nice to go out and hang out with people, instead of sitting in her apartment with Robusta, watching TV and overthinking every little thing. She was finally starting to make some progress with her financial situation and might soon own her roastery building. This was all new.

She flattened a piece of her orange hair on the top of her head and looked over her face, lightly dotted with freckles, green eyes prominent. She heaved a nervous sigh, washed her hands, and headed back out to the table. As she was navigating around the tables, she spotted someone familiar across the room. Everywhere in this town there was bound to be someone familiar, but this was a face that was familiar in the wrong context.

It was one of the table bussers. The blonde, tousled hair of the middle-aged man shimmered under the amber hanging light of The Diner as he turned with the bus tub full of dishes and headed back for the kitchen. She rushed back to the table.

"What is Michael doing bussing tables?" she asked, just above a whisper. Josie turned her head to look behind her. "Don't loook." Clementine fussed, though Michael was already in the back.

"What's wrong with this guy having a … job?" Simon asked, taking a drink of his water.

"Michael owns the local boutique up the street. Why and how does he have time to have a second job—let alone one at Brent's restaurant?" It donned on her. Her eyes glazed over. "I wonder…" she trailed off. "I wonder if Brent got to Michael the way he tried with me!" She was in her own mind now, her thoughts running a million miles a second.

"What do you mean?" Simon asked again, scratching his chin, his brow furrowed.

She leaned into the table, her voice lowered. "Well, Brent is this big, cocky business mogul, right? Michael probably borrowed money from him, and now he has to pay him back somehow so Brent is making him work in his diner to pay back his debt. It's like striking a deal with the devil. Brent is on some vendetta to buy all the buildings up in Roastwood Hollow. He tried coming for me. Cornered me in the bank. I have suspicions that he could possibly—"

"Clem, the waitress came when you were gone and I ordered that sandwich for you. Did you want anything else?" Josie reached for a napkin and started twisting it in her hands.

Clementine pursed her lips, her cheeks burning as she placed her hands in her lap. She couldn't even make eye contact with Simon. She'd gone too far. She couldn't help it.

"Are you serious, Clementine?" It was a rhetorical question with a strict tone. He hadn't used her full name like that since he'd gotten comfortable with her. She wasn't sure how she felt about that.

"Please do not tell me we are here so that you can check up on him."

"No—I really did want you to experience it!" She didn't even sound natural saying it. Josie knew she couldn't stand the guy and there were so many other local spots they could have gone instead. Clementine felt like a child being scolded by her parents.

"I thought I told you to back off!" Simon threw his own napkin down and pushed his chair back.

"Don't go, Simon."

He shook his head. "This ... this stuff is out of your wheelhouse. It's dangerous. It's not smart for you to continue investigating this case. Let it go, Clem." He swept his gaze across the other tables, as they were drawing attention.

Josie sat back, unwilling to get involved. Clem could tell her friend was uncomfortable, and it made her stomach churn. She mouthed 'I'm sorry' to her and turned back to Simon. "I shouldn't have said all that," she said quietly, avoiding his gaze.

"I just... need some air." He shook his head again and took off toward the entrance of the diner.

Clementine looked at Josie apologetically.

"I mean… I can't help it. I feel like the police are either hiding something, or they are incompetent. And Simon just wants to fit in, because he's new and in training. He doesn't want to skip a beat. So I have to do *something*. Also, why is Michael working here, when he owns his own business—that's weird, right?"

Josie nodded, quiet a moment, and then she responded. "It's weird."

The waitress approached their table, laying down the plates of food. "Does everything look good? Can I get you all anything else?"

"No, this is perfect, Doris. Thank you." Clementine smiled and the waitress took off. "Should I go get him?" she asked.

Josie shrugged.

"He'll come back… right? He seemed pretty angry. He can't prove that's what I'm doing here. There's nothing wrong with going out to eat somewhere and being… observant?" She laughed under her breath.

Josie took a bite of her salad and shrugged.

"What?" Clementine shot back, avoiding her eye contact. She picked up her sandwich, bursting with roast beef on the sides, with both hands.

"You were a *little* unhinged." Josie demonstrated by pinching her thumb and pointer finger together in front of her squinted face. "Seems to me like he's worried about you.

Concerned for your safety. There's something to be said for that."

"Ooorr he doesn't trust me."

"Well, it's not your job to be an investigator."

"You're right. It's not. It's their job. And they're not doing their job. According to the captain at the community meeting, it seemed like they're only concerned about the Snowflake Festival. And if Paul didn't take his own life, which I suspect he didn't, then that means there's still a killer on the loose. And I want to roast my coffee without fear that I'm next. And I don't want anybody else in this town to get hurt either."

Josie looked back and forth, her eyes wide. "Shhh... Clem."

Clementine looked around. Everyone had gone back to what they were doing and seemed only interested in their own worlds anyway. "Nobody's listening..." she said quietly.

"It's Roastwood. Somebody is allllways listening," Josie urged.

Clementine smirked and pushed her chair back. Okay, Josie wasn't wrong. "I'm gonna go get him. His food will get cold." She stood and headed for the door. She put both hands on the door and pushed into the outside. A chill had picked up in the air, and she shielded her eyes from the wind as she peered out, but Simon wasn't standing right outside. She heard a voice at the edge of the building. As she went nearer, she heard him talking, likely on the phone as it sounded one-sided. For a moment, she thought to burst around the corner, but then his words caught her attention.

"All I'm saying is, we should be giving it another look. It's not ethical to receive information from an autopsy and not use it to re-open a decision already made."

She could sense his frustration.

"No! I'm not saying we release it to the public. That's the least of my worries."

Clementine leaned against the wall a moment, soaking in guilt. Simon *was* fighting for what she'd been pushing for, for them to investigate the Paul case even farther. He wasn't failing to try because he was new. Perhaps the nepotism protected him, even if his dad was retired or worked for a different precinct. Or, perhaps he was just a decent guy. She hadn't expected this curveball. Her cheeks flushed as she leaned her head back on the brick wall. She felt bad she'd held any ill feelings towards him, and that she was listening in.

"Yeah, no, I'll drive by their house to see if I can pick anything else up. It was interesting that the forensics team recovered that evidence at the scene. It just gives us one more person to look into. No, I appreciate it."

One more person to look into. Did they have another suspect? Her stomach somersaulted as the cadence of the conversation trended towards ending. Right when she was about to propel herself away from the building and into the alley, Simon appeared.

"Later—what in the—" He'd hung up the phone and turned the corner, running right into her.

Clementine shuddered, backing into the wall once more.

"How long were you standing here?" His eyes narrowed. "Were you listening?"

She deserved the accusatory tone.

"No! I mean, I came out here to let you know our food was out and I didn't want yours to get cold. I may… I may have heard a little bit of your conversation."

He sighed, shaking his head and scratching the back of his neck. "This is… Clem this is too much. It's dangerous for you to be involved." He pointed at her. "I have told you time and time again."

Now, she didn't like his tone. He was treating her like a little kid.

"Got it. Loud and clear," she said, throwing her hands up and turning away from him to march back inside. She hated this feeling. The night was not supposed to go down like that. She arrived back at the table. Josie was nearly finished with her meal, and looked up at the two of them as though caught red-handed with a full mouth. After she swallowed, she blinked. "How nice of you two to join me." She smirked, though the tone did not meet her there.

"I think it's best if I just get a doggy bag," Simon said quietly, standing next to his chair.

Clementine plopped herself down in her own chair. She rubbed her biceps and avoided eye contact with Simon.

"Oh? Didn't go well…out there?" Josie asked, eyebrows raised, looking from Simon to Clem and back again.

"Yeah, something came up. Enjoy your night, girls."

Clementine nodded, still looking away as Simon grabbed his plate and took it up to the bar counter. He was gone as quickly as he'd come.

Well, it was nobody's fault but her own that she had friend-zoned him immediately. He did ask her to dinner. Just her. And she showed up with a friend. Ultimate friend-zone move. But she was focused on trying to figure out who did this crime, and gaining back her sense of comfort, since everything in her life had been uprooted.

If nobody else was going to make it a priority, she had to bring Paul's killer to justice, regardless of what relationship she had with the man. He was still her landlord, and she felt like she paid overpriced rent monthly for him to not help fix anything. But his family was willing to work with her, and give her a path to stability. If the murderer had killed Paul in the interest of getting his buildings and assets, like Brent was leading her to believe, then that is where she needed to stay. And apparently, according to Simon's call outside, evidence was found at the scene that could potentially lead to another suspect. Perhaps that suspect was Brent. She was almost certain of that. But if it wasn't him, then she needed to find out who that other suspect was.

"Earth to Clementine…" Josie sang, waving her hands in front of Clem's face. "What did you do to him out there?" she joked.

"Yeah. I eavesdropped on his private conversation on the phone, and he's upset that I'm still poking my nose in the case."

"Well, you are."

"I know that! But I have to."

"We all just want you to be careful. Yes, that includes me."

"Well, help me then."

Josie put her fork down with a clang against the plate. "Even though Simon told you to back off, you're not gonna, are you?"

Clementine stared at Josie, her eyes twinkling.

"So what's next then?"

"Tomorrow afternoon, between lunch and dinner rush, when Brent is out of his office, I'm going to go bug it, and see if I can get any more information from in there. It'd be nice if you wanted to help. Be the lookout?"

"You certainly can't ask your cop friend to help, now can you? Sounds totally illegal, Clem."

"So is murder." Clementine poked at her sandwich, her stomach in knots.

"Touché. Fine, I'll come. But I do have a shipment coming to the cafe in the morning."

"Sounds like a plan." Maybe not a very good one. And definitely one that cost her a relationship that was just forming with Simon, but she had more pressing matters at hand.

"You should try the chickpea salad wrap."

Clementine looked up from her plate to see Polly wafting by, wearing a flowy skirt.

"We're *done* eating." Josie chimed in.

"Next time, next time." Polly said, leaning over the bar counter.

Clementine chuckled, pushing the tension

far down in her body. "What're you doing here, Polly?"

Polly looked over her shoulder, "Just grabbing drinks before I head out to a meeting at the Nature Preserve."

"Oh, good luck with that." Clementine turned back to Josie and the table. She pushed her plate forward to signify she was done.

"That girl is everywhere. Does she ever sleep?" Josie asked Clem.

Clem shook her head. " Your guess is as good as mine. I'll go look for Doris, so we can get to-go boxes and the check. We're going to need to get home and get some sleep before what's to come."

"Aye aye, detective." Josie made a face that could only be described as 'you're crazy', but she was still a good enough friend to lend a hand. Josie and Clementine had worked the espresso bar together on a Saturday morning back in the day, and if they could do that, then they could do anything.

CHAPTER
NINE

Clementine sat in the coffeehouse booth, a mug of drip coffee in front of her, mostly to look like she had a purpose for being there. She tapped her foot, all of her nerves building the longer she sat. She looked up at Josie, who was working behind the counter, making drinks at the bar and greeting customers as they walked in.

She was lucky and happy she'd made the decision to go into business with Josie. They'd met at this shop years ago, and she couldn't imagine doing this with anybody else. Owning a business together was like a marriage. Business partners need complete trust in each other. Josie and Clementine had to give each other access to all of their finances, credit scores, assets and liabilities; they had to put up equal collateral, go to the bank together, and get a loan. It was a huge deal.

Clem had lucked out scoring the roasting portion of the business. She'd done the coffee-house for many years as a barista, but roasting was less customer-facing, which fueled her introverted heart. And she didn't have to worry about the overhead that Josie did. She could just go back to her facility and be in her own little world, focusing on her craft and being a technician. Most importantly, Clementine didn't have to worry about labor and staffing, something that had become much more of a challenge than she ever thought it'd be. It seemed as though nobody wanted to work, but everyone wanted money. Even though she didn't have to deal with that first hand, she did hear about it a lot from Josie.

Soon, she would likely need to hire an assistant roaster, but for now she was happy with Robusta as her companion at the roasting facility. She was on the cusp of landing new clients and getting busier, but she could handle the work on her own—when she wasn't having to solve crimes, of course.

Clem took a sip of the coffee, the familiar warmth sliding down her throat and calming her nerves. She put her bag up on the table and fumbled inside it for the device she'd picked up at the store before coming here. She didn't have time to go onto a spy website and order one of their devices, so she had to settle for finding this one in person.

Before she moved to Roastwood Hollow, there was a strip mall near her house. It wasn't the nicest of areas. It had a dodgy looking massage parlor, a liquor store, a boutique that looked like it sold clothing for working girls. On the corner was a quirky little store that advertised ninja stars, pepper spray, the works: a self-defense store. Clementine remembered seeing that they also sold security devices.

It wasn't far from Roastwood Hollow, so she had taken a trip there this morning and purchased a recording device that looked like a regular flash drive: something that could be found in any office, since that's where she would be planting it. The good thing about going out of her comfort zone and into a store like that—one that she was always curious about, because it was so peculiar—was that they didn't ask any questions. Your business was your own; it was basically their motto. It worked in her favor, that's for sure.

The plan was simple. Go to Brent's office and plant a recording device hidden in plain sight. If he came back while she was placing it, she'd come up with a quick excuse why she was there. For instance, she could bait him by saying she wanted to discuss his offer more.

That would definitely distract him from the fact that she was putting a bug in his office.

Nowadays, they made all kinds of recording devices in disguise. There were flash drives, pens, recorders the size of a coin. It was pretty easy to make it undetectable. She glanced at the flash drive once more and tucked it back inside her bag.

"How's the coffee?"

Clem jerked her head up to see Josie standing by the table, pulling her apron off over her head.

"Oh it's great! You know I need to try it now and then for quality control reasons."

Josie laughed. "Of course. Even though you're the one that calibrates the brewer over here."

"Well… you never know if the barista has measured out the proper amount of beans."

"Mm hm… no, it's cool. Did you get the thing? You ready?"

"Oh, I got the thing." She patted her bag. "And I'm nervous as heck."

Josie walked back behind the counter again and hooked her apron up. "Hey, I'll be back in a little bit!" she called over to the two baristas in the kitchen washing dishes. "Let's go. I've got your back."

Clem shuffled out of the booth, throwing the bag over her shoulder. She finished off the coffee and placed the mug into the bus tub gingerly before leaving the coffeehouse with Josie.

"Just remember," Josie said, "act like you are where you're supposed to be, and nobody will be suspicious. Totally normal. Nobody will question us two walking through Roast-wood, or going into Brent's office. It could happen any day, right?" She patted Clem on the back of the shoulder as they walked.

"Josie?" Clem asked.

"Hm?"

"Your talking is making me more ner-vous." She laughed under her breath, which fogged in the air because of the chill.

"Sorry, you know I talk when I'm nervous."

"We can't *both* be nervous! You acted back there like this was a piece of cake!"

They both laughed. "Well you know, fake it till you make it. The stakes are pretty high here. You're trying to catch a literal murderer."

They rounded the corner and walked past the doors of The Diner. Brent's office door was just down the side of the building on the right. When they got to the door, Clementine glanced into the side window. If Brent happened to be there, she had her cover story. She came up with a backup story about some gift card promo Main Street was doing. Even though, the last thing she wanted was to talk to him. At least she'd have Josie with her. Perhaps he wouldn't use his body to pin her into a corner to try and intimidate her.

"Looks like he's not in there. He's gone," Clem said, tugging on the door. "Locked! Of course, why wouldn't it be?" She looked at Josie, then their surroundings, to make sure nobody else was watching them.

"Okay, hold on. Stay here," Josie stated confidently.

"Wait! I don't want to be a sitting duck!" Clem threw her hands up.

"Well then come back with me and wait outside the door. I'm going into The Diner."

Clementine almost protested, but she shut her mouth and followed Josie. She had no choice. They'd hit a wall in their plan, one they clearly should have thought about prior to setting out on this journey, but some things just can't be planned for. This one was a roadblock, but not the end of it. Worse things could have happened. Like, he could have actually been inside his office, requiring her to have a conversation with him.

"Stay here." Josie pointed to the spot next to the diner door, swung the door open, and headed inside with a jingle of the bell.

Clem kicked her foot back and forth,

leaning against the stone wall by the door. She wrinkled her nose at the smell of some residual cigarette smoke in the air. Clem scanned the buildings on the Main Street of Roastwood Hollow. White lights trimmed each of the buildings, one after the other on both ends of the street. Banners hung on the vintage-style light poles, showcasing the up-coming Snowflake Festival. She remembered the meeting where they had argued and agreed upon a design for the banners. It was always something.

"Score!" Josie leaped back out of the diner with a ring of keys, holding and isolating one large gold key.

"How did you—?"

"Sarah's working today." Sarah was one of the managers that had been working at The Diner for Brent for nearly seventeen years. Clementine had no idea how Sarah had lasted that long. They started walking back down the side of the building toward the office door.

Josie spoke just above a whisper to Clementine, so they weren't airing out their business for someone to eavesdrop. "I told her we borrowed something from Brent for the shop and I needed to return it, but he wasn't there. She said she'd come let me in, but they were slammed in there and short-staffed, a likely story. So I told her that I'd run in there real quick and then bring her back the key."

They approached the door. "But wait, shouldn't we leave something then? In case Sarah tells Brent you came for the key or something? We have to make our story make sense."

Josie fumbled with the key a moment at the door. "You're right... uhhh."

Clementine thought about it. "Wait! I have a bag of the Christmas coffee blend in my backpack right now. I was bringing it home for my home supply, but we could put it on Brent's desk. If she asks if our story checks out, we could say that you said it was something you borrowed only because you wanted to surprise him? Leave me out of this, please." She chuckled, playfully hitting Josie on the arm. "Just say it's from the shop."

Josie laughed, looked back and forth, and then put the key in the slot. She opened the door, and they both shuffled in.

"I'll wait at the door and you do your thing, okay?"

Clementine nodded, then dug into her backpack for both the flash drive recording device and the bag of coffee. She set the coffee on his desk so that he would see it right away, then she searched around for a good place to plant the device. Somewhere it would be overlooked…

She spotted a basket on the bookshelf behind the desk that sported paper boxes, likely containing vendor invoices and paperwork to close out bookkeeping. It looked familiar to how she did her own books—the old fashioned way. She also had digital books, but there was nothing like keeping physical records. It was still a must. Even though she was young, she clung to some dated methods, like writing checks several times a week for her business. Some of the coffeehouse baristas didn't even know how to write a check, or own any checks to provide for their direct deposit. But surely there were things from her parents' generation that she had no idea how to do as well.

She dropped the flash drive recording device into the basket with the pens, chargers, and other tech stuff and hurried back to the door.

"I think it's good. I don't want to stay here any longer." She tapped on Josie's back for her to get a move on. Being there gave her the creeps.

They left the office, locking it behind them.

"I'm going to go give Sarah her keys back. You want me to pick up a drink to share and head to your place?"

Clementine nodded. "Yes, absolutely. Can I help cover it?"

Josie looked down at her phone, then back to Clem. "No, I have tips from that wedding we catered the other day." She placed her hand on the door of the diner.

"Okay cool, drive safe and see you soon." Clementine started to walk away, down the cobblestone street. She looked over her shoulder and called out as they parted ways. "Oh and Josie? Thank you. Best accomplice I could ever ask for."

"Shh!" Josie responded with her index finger to her lips, laughing. She exaggeratingly looked around before slipping back into the diner with the key.

Clementine returned the laugh, loaded with nerves and overwhelmed with triumph, and took off down the other way, back toward the roastery where her car was parked.

Clementine just got settled on her couch, when her phone dinged with a text from Josie stating 'here'. She scrambled off the seat and moseyed over to the door in her fuzzy socks and sweats, looked through the peephole in the door, and pulled it open.

Josie stood on the landing, her curly hair

looking more untamed than ever, and held up the bottle of deep red Tawny Port, a sweet dessert wine. "Nightcap?"

"Yes, please." Clementine motioned her into the apartment and closed the door behind her. "It's been too long since we've gotten the chance to do something not work-related."

"And you need to get some of that tension out. I gave you your space after Paul's murder, but now I'm not going anywhere." Josie made a beeline for the kitchen.

If Clementine was the hugging type, this is where she'd initiate that. Alas, she nodded at Josie, appreciating her more than she knew. "Thank you…" she trailed off. "Cups!" Clem turned and followed her to the kitchen, which was only steps away considering she lived in a one bedroom apartment. She reached up to the exposed floating shelves and pulled two glasses, bringing them to the counter.

"Cortado glasses?" Josie laughed, un-screwing the lid to the port.

"It's just the vessel to get the liquid into my face." The last thing Clem wanted to do was get Josie worked up about glasses. She recalled the time they were taking inventory at the shop and Josie went into the science of latte cups and their aromatic properties.

She poured up the port into both glasses

and handed one to Josie, then headed back over to the couch.

"So today was pretty crazy, huh? How much time do you think we should give it before we go retrieve the recording device?" Josie joined her on the couch.

Clem brought the glass to her lips and took a sip. Richly sweet wine, with a pleasant burn in her throat at the finish. "Oh, right. We have to go get it back." She palmed her forehead. "You think maybe a couple of days?"

Josie nodded, sipping her port as well. "Definitely before the Snowflake Festival. Otherwise we'll get swept up by the chaos surrounding the festival."

"Very true. But no more shop talk." Clementine laughed.

"You're right. So how's the cop? Did you make up?"

Clem's eyes glazed over. She deadpanned, "Okay… let's go back to talking about the shop."

Both girls laughed.

Clementine took another sip from the glass, then placed it on the monstera-shaped coffee table next to the couch. "For real though, I think he just wants space. He hasn't reached out, though neither have I. He was upset because he thought I was poking around the case—"

"—Which you are."

"Shhh." Clem put her index finger to her lips.

"Okay, okay. For real though, back to the coffeehouse for just a moment," Josie started. "I wanted to let you know that should you decide not to move forward with purchasing the building from Paul's family, or if it falls through or something, there will always be space for you at the coffeehouse. I know it's small for a roaster, but we can make it work. I don't want you to have to worry about that."

Clem's chest warmed, and not just from the port. She was at a loss for words, but nodded. "You're the best."

"d'awe, thanks." She gently patted the side of Clem's arm.

Clementine reached over and picked up her glass again, finishing it off. Then, she searched for the bottle.

"Okay, enough of the mushy talk. Where's that beardy…" Josie stood. "I need cuddles."

CHAPTER
TEN

The next day, Clementine heaved a huge yawn as she finished sticking labels onto the coffee bags. She moved them to the next prep table gingerly. Her head swooned; seemed she had a bit more to drink last night than intended. Nothing a little espresso couldn't fix. Although her evening with Josie was a much needed reprieve from the tension she'd been basking in daily, she couldn't get her mind off of the work she had ahead of her today. And no, she wasn't thinking about the work at the roastery.

She went over again in her mind yesterday's spy work in Brent's office. She wasn't sure what she'd do with the recorded proof, if she acquired it, since it had been captured illegally; but it would at least give her an answer. And luckily, Josie was willing to help.

She filled each coffee bag with the amount of beans needed. Then she moved it over to the heat sealer, placing the bag in between the heating elements, and stepping down on the foot lever to melt the two sides of the bag together. Then, she set each bag down on the counter to date them with the label gun. It was monotonous work, and she much preferred the actual art of roasting. When they had more orders than she could handle, which happened from time to time, she would borrow somebody from Josie's shop to help her with the postproduction, just to make things easier.

Clementine didn't like the monotonous. She didn't like routine. She was a fast mover, and loved filling her time with things to do. That's why her time at home after the incident with Paul was so anxiety-inducing. She had so much time to think about all the possibilities, and all the ways she could be in danger. That's what motivated her to get a move on. She didn't want to see anyone else in this town injured or dead.

After she finished with the last bag and packaged them up in the boxes, she swung her black bomber jacket onto her body and grabbed her backpack. She checked her phone for the time, turned off the lights in the roasting facility, and made her way to the door. After locking it behind her, she turned and shuddered with a start. She'd run right into Polly rushing towards her, the small town's executive director.

"Clementine!" She exclaimed, as Clem composed herself.

"You were so quiet, I didn't even hear you!" Clem said, brushing off her fright and backing up from her. "Sorry, I was just locking up."

"Going somewhere in a hurry?"

Clementine tried to decide if she wanted to lie or not. "Yeah, maybe you can come with me and we can chat. I'm headed to Brent's office." *Why did she say that?* She kicked herself inside. It was the first thing she thought to say, probably because it was constantly on her mind.

"No! Wait… Uhh." Polly stiffened, appearing uncomfortable and defensive. She grabbed Clementine's arm, hard.

Clem shook off her hand, then made eye contact, startled by her reaction.

"Uhh, I just came from there. It's not… it's not—" Her voice was uncharacteristically high.

"What's going on, Polly?"

"Brent is dead."

Clementine's heart felt like it stopped in her chest, her whole body trembling. "What?"

She had heard Polly. But she was in disbelief. "How—how do you know?"

"I went to Brent's office to talk to him about a donation for the Snowflake Festival, and found it swarming with police," her voice trembled. "So I peeked in his office…"

"Polly?"

"I had nothing to do with this, if that's what you are accusing, Clem!" She brushed her palms on her pants.

Clem cocked an eyebrow. "I wasn't accusing anything. I'm just… I'm in shock, that's all." She pulled off her backpack and placed it on the sidewalk. Then she sat on the bench next to the roastery door and placed her head in her hands. Her thoughts raced. If police were swarming, then Josie would have seen them and texted Clementine to tell her the plan was off. But she didn't have any texts from Josie. *Was Polly lying?*

Clementine stood again. "We have to go there!"

"I won't go anywhere near there!"

"Wait… why did you come here? Were you coming to get me?"

Polly held her arm to her chest as though something was bothering her.

"Are you injured?" Clementine narrowed her eyes.

"No, I'm fine, I'm fine. I just came here to

talk to you about your donation to the Snowflake Festival and where you wanted to place your tent for the coffee… and also just thought you should know about Brent."

Clem pulled her jacket together in front, shivering from more than the chill in the air.

"Did you… did you want to donate a portion of the coffee for the festival?"

Clementine's hand rose to land on her hip. "Polly!"

"What!? I'm sorry, I'm so anxious."

"Brent just *died*! And all you care about is this festival!"

"I just default to being busy when I don't want to think about scary things." She put her hands up in surrender.

"That's two community members that have died in a short period of time. Is it connected with Paul? Did you see anything or ask any questions?" A part of Clementine felt suspicious of Polly. She knew Brent was dead, but there wasn't anything else out about it yet. Would police even give up that kind of information? How did Polly know so much, if she hadn't been involved in it herself?

Perhaps…perhaps Polly should be added to her suspect list. Which was convenient, considering Clem's number one suspect had just been murdered. She'd have to go back to the drawing board yet again, and the tension was high. If it hadn't been confirmed before, if she'd had any doubts a killer was on the loose, it was now concrete that was exactly what was happening ... right?

"Okay Polly, well I'm not going to stay here at the roastery alone like a sitting duck, so I'm going to the coffee shop. Thanks for the heads up. Uhhh, for the festival, just whatever the organization needs. I can donate half, that's fine."

"Oh thanks, Clem. That's perfect. I'll get out of your hair. Hey, if I find any more information about what happened, I'll be sure to let you know!"

Clementine smiled. "Okay, thank you." She nodded and took off in the direction of the shop, eager to get away from Polly.

Walking briskly along the sidewalk, she kept her attention on all her surroundings. A few squad cars were left in front of the office of The Diner, which appeared to be running as usual. She wasn't sure if his staff even knew. Surely if Polly was already out telling neighboring small businesses then Brent's staff should know. However, he had a full team working the place when he wasn't there, and the police may have thought it best if everything operated as usual to not raise an alarm. Both scenarios seemed logical.

If only she wasn't half-convinced that

Simon never wanted to talk to her again, she could have called him. She rounded the corner and bolted straight for the coffeehouse. Roastwood Coffee sat on the historic Main Street in all of its glory. It was swarming with all the usual townsfolk that frequented the shop. A main accessory to its exterior was the old man and his equally old scraggly dog sitting on the bench outside. They'd put out a water bowl by the door to the shop specifically for the grumpy old man dog. Not the old man, who was kind as can be and often enjoyed talking about various works of literature. The old man's dog, on the other hand, had taken enough of everyone's crap and wasn't afraid to let you know it. Clem chuckled to herself as she reached for the door, relishing in the normalcy that the coffeehouse brought her every time she stepped foot in it.

The familiar bells dinged as she stepped inside out of the brisk air. The warmth of the coffeehouse embraced her, inviting with smells of cinnamon and sweet bread.

She walked past the register and rounded behind the counter. Pulling a mug from the warm top of the brewer, she poured herself a cup from the coffee pot and checked the sign to see which roast they had on tap. It was a Honduras, one that she'd roasted just four days ago. She closed her eyes and stuck her nose into the cup, inhaling the steam that wafted up. It was simply perfect. So perfect, she'd nearly tuned out all the other baristas behind the counter.

She didn't see Josie at the moment, which wasn't out of the ordinary. Josie was probably in the basement of the shop working on the night drop deposit.

Clem nodded to a barista at the sink, elbow deep in dishes. "How's it going in here today?" she asked another barista at the bar. A sudden tightening gripped her throat. She inhaled the coffee steam again as a heat rose from the back of her neck. It felt wrong to just pretend everything was normal: as if another community member hadn't just been murdered across the street. Her gaze flicked over the front door, then down to her shoes.

"Not too bad. Something going on out there?" The curly-haired barista gestured to the front door. He finished pouring the milk from the pitcher and lidded the cup, then put it on the counter. "Vanilla latte for Stella!"

"Yeah, definitely. But I'm not entirely sure what just yet. Josie downstairs?"

"No, actually. She texted and said she'd be in later because she didn't sleep well last night." He wiped the counter with a paper towel and tossed it in the trash.

"Okay, thanks. I'm out of here." She slipped her phone out of her pocket with her free hand and checked the time. "Good job on the brew." She held up her mug to hypothetical cheers it and then took off.

Clementine took her mug of coffee and headed back out of the coffeehouse, up the street and into her car. She sipped the coffee and placed her mug into the car cup holder and retrieved her phone. She didn't end things well the last time she saw Simon. She needed him, now more than ever, after a second killing. If someone was going building to building in this small town and killing people, who's to say she wasn't next? As much as she complained about the gossip in this town, she cared about everyone that was in it.

When she thought about the two killings, she couldn't find any connection between Paul and Brent besides that they both lived in Roastwood Hollow. Of course, there was the possibility that the building tied them together.

Paul owned the building.

Paul died.

Paul's family was in the process of selling said building to her.

Brent wanted the building.

Did somebody want the building more than Brent, and find out he was inquiring about it? How could they know that he had those intentions?

Who knew that Brent had approached her, and with what…

Greg at the bank? Greg knew about the conversation. He'd rescued her from it. But surely Greg wasn't a killer…

She needed to sit and think about every single person that had been in that community meeting. It could be anyone.

Polly.

Sandy the bank teller.

An inside police job? That could be the reason it seemed they didn't want to investigate further into Paul's murder.

Could it have been an outside person altogether, just terrorizing the small river town?

She was digging a hole sitting in that car, deeper and deeper. She stared at the phone, then tapped on the number from her recents.

No answer. Voicemail. Judging by the amount of times it rang, she couldn't help but think he silenced the call and sent it to voicemail. "Simon…" she whispered, setting her phone on the passenger seat.

She rested her hands on ten and two and replayed the interaction she'd had with Polly outside the roastery over and over in her head. Surely authorities were swarming

Brent's office by now. They'd likely tear the place apart. No doubt they'd find…

"My recording device," she heaved into the silent car. Her heart palpitated for a moment. There's no way they'd be able to trace it back to her. It was quite generic. But… it could have potentially recorded Brent's murder. Why wasn't Simon answering his phone?

She needed a game plan.

The Snowflake Festival was just around the corner. The town would be featured on a pedestal. It was the next opportunity where the whole town would be in one place at one time. The perfect place to spot a killer.

She started the engine and took off toward home.

CHAPTER
ELEVEN

The key jammed in the dead bolt. Clem put her shoulder into the door and jiggled the key while turning the knob, then pushed into the roastery. She set Robusta down and the little bearded dragon took off to do her rounds. Clementine stood a moment in the doorway, scanning the dark building in the red glow of the exit sign above the door. She walked into the facility and flipped the light switch.

She squinted a moment, sensitive to the illuminated overhead lights.

She moseyed over to the roaster and flipped on the drum first, then the blower, then the pilot light for the gas. Once ignited, she switched the pilot to the burners. The heating element underneath the drum fired up. She peered into the window and watched the burners ignite from the pilot, first in all blue fire, the hottest, then waving down to an orange red. It was her favorite part of the process. There was something so warm and cozy about the coffee roaster firing up, knowing the aroma of comfort would soon follow.

Next came measuring the green coffee beans. She walked to the counter with the scale, burlap sacks filled with green coffee piled beside it. She looked over her shoulder to see Robusta slowly waddling back into the main room and settling in her favorite spot by the window. She wondered if Robusta had any thoughts about what had happened in this building the last time she was here, or if she just enjoyed her snacks and bugs. Did bearded dragons have a memory like that?

Everything seemed to go according to plan. She measured the beans and brought them over to the roaster, which was nearly preheated for charging the beans into the hopper above. Every time she pulled that lever to release the beans into the drum, she felt a major accomplishment, like 'And they're off!'. The beans would always make the same shaking sound in the drum, like a maraca.

Roasting coffee was an immersive process requiring the use of many senses. Smell to know which stage of development she was in, especially the 'yellowing phase', which smelled of sweet bread. Sight when using the trier, the device that pulled a small sampling of beans from the drum while they cooked. It was essential to check what they looked like and compare the beans to past batches for color, size, and development. And finally, hearing to listen for when the first crack happened, which made a very audible popping sound.

Clementine looked at the clipboard on the cart next to the roaster to make sure her timing and temperature were lining up with the flavor profile. The digital thermometer read a temperature higher than it should have. She furrowed her brow and checked all of the variables and controls.

Quickly, she pulled the trier out of the face of the roaster to check the beans. The vapors wafting from the beans in the trier were more intense than it should have been at this point in the roast. Her first response was to turn the gas flame all the way down to zero, leaving just the pilot light remaining. Judging by the stagnant and then increasing hand on the manometer, the gauge that showed gas input, turning the gas off was not working. She turned off the pilot light, frantically looking over each control.

"What in the…" She looked over her

shoulder at the door. Robusta's harness jingled as she stood from her nap on the windowsill at the ready.

"Robusta... I don't know what's happening," she whined over to her companion. "This has never happened before." The empty roastery echoed back her words. Through the viewing hole at the heating element, it appeared the dial for her gas input was not working. She looked at the roaster, then to the door again. "Okay... okay." Her heart raced and breath caught. She bolted to the door, swung it open, and walked away from the building, looking up. She put her hand to her forehead to shield her eyes from the sun as the chimney ducting came into view, vapors pouring into the sky. It was not good.

Black billowing smoke.

The absolute last thing a roaster wants to see in the middle of a batch is black smoke. Smoke meant fire, somewhere in either the ducting or the drum. She'd never had this happen before, though she'd trained on what to do. The pounding of her heart inside her chest was unreal. She ran back inside the roastery, Robusta at her ankles. She picked up her phone on the cart by the tracking clipboard.

She contemplated whether to call 911. Call

the fire department. Call Simon. What if the fire got out of control? She couldn't cut the electrical power to the roaster. If she did that, the drum would immediately stop. At such a high temperature, the drum could warp. And her very expensive asset, the foundation of her business, would be done. Her business would be done. It wouldn't even matter if she'd been granted first dibs on the building.

She also couldn't let the beans out of the drum, because she hadn't been able to locate the source of the fire yet. If the fire was inside the drum with the coffee, and judging by the smell of the beans, there was a fair chance of that, then if she let the beans into the cooling bin, the fire would come out with it.

Just then, an alarm blared out of the roaster. Her hands cupped her ears. She'd never heard the alarm before despite reading about it in the manual. It went off when the roaster reached temperatures internally around 480 degrees Fahrenheit. The manual warned that if it were to hit 500 degrees, then the whole roaster could catch fire and blow up, essentially. That was her ultimate fear. Despite reading about it, she could have never prepared for the sheer loudness of it, on top of the echoey atmosphere of the roastery itself.

She couldn't use her fire extinguisher on

the wall either because it would also ruin her machine. "Robusta, go!" Clementine shouted over the sound of the roaster's motors and the blaring alarm. "Go back in the window!" She moved her gently with her foot.

She didn't want to call the fire department, because she was worried that they would do something to compromise her machine.

"Okay. Figure this... out," she told herself out loud. "You have no other choice."

She rounded the back of the roaster, near its rear ducting, and eyed the gas line on the wall. When she'd had it installed, she had them put in a shut-off valve there for this exact reason. It was so that she didn't have to run out to the back of the building if she ever needed to cut the gas input into her machine. She cranked the shutoff valve counter clockwise, straining and letting out a grunt as she closed off the line. She rounded the roaster again and looked into the view hole.

The smell of the coffee well past its time reminded her of two other times. First, when she had seasoned the roaster. The drum was made of material similar to a cast iron skillet; when brand new, it needed to be seasoned by roasting coffee in its own residual heat for a long period of time.

The second time was the evening that Paul was murdered.

The view hole didn't show any signs of fire and was mostly dark, so she put her hand on the lever that opened the drum into the cooling bin. She switched the toggle for the agitator and adjusted the airflow to pull air through in the cooling bin. She stopped for a moment with her hand clutching the lever, put her forehead against her hand, closed her eyes, and took a deep breath. "Breathe…" she whispered. Then she stood back at the ready and pulled the lever.

Black charcoaled beans spilled out of the drum and into the cooling bin, spinning with the agitator. She closed her eyes and yanked her face back away from the steam that enveloped her. After all the coffee was out, she took the trier and propped it into the roasting drum door, allowing heat to continue to escape the drum. She also left the hopper door open to invite more air in. She held her breath as she glanced over at the digital temperature reading and heaved a huge sigh. It was trending down. She placed her hand on her chest, "Oh thank goodness," she declared out into the empty roasting facility.

After she caught her breath, she stood back from the roaster and grabbed her cell phone.

"Hello? Hi, yes this is Clementine Matthews with Roastwood Coffee. I was wondering if you could send someone to come check out my gas line?"

"Do you smell natural gas within the building?" the operator asked.

"No, no, I just had a surge of gas in my... roaster." She didn't want to tip them off that there had been a fire in her roaster because it got too hot. "I had an issue when I was roasting coffee with the gas input, but the problem resolved when I turned the shut-off inside my building."

"We'll send someone over right away, Ms. Matthews. Hang tight."

"Thank you." She hung up with dispatch and heaved another large sigh, reaching down and picking up Robusta for the first time. She hugged the reptile to her chest. She put Robusta back down and leaned over the cooling bin, resting both hands on the rim. The burnt coffee beans swiveled around the center, toppling over each other clockwise, pushed by the little agitator paddles. All of the coffee beans were a similar color, just black. Usually they were light to dark brown, some with marbling. Never this black. This was going to be a wasted batch, something that rarely happened in her many years of experience roasting.

As she watched the beans, something caught her eye.

It was silver and shimmering among the black beans, the contrast striking. By now, the coffee, if you could even call it that, was cool enough to touch. She dipped her hand in and let the beans fall back into the bin, missing the silver piece that had caught her eye. She continued to stare at the beans as they spun. Occasionally there was a piece of debris that would end up in the beans at the source, missing the quality control checks. Normally it was rocks, pieces of concrete or volcanic. Sometimes a spare bolt or screw would get in there. That's what this must have been, based on the shiny silver color.

It surfaced again, and she scooped up a large double handful this time, the beans sprawling down from her hands back into the cooling bin. As the beans fell away, the culprit surfaced in her palm.

She froze.

Her hands began to shake and she struggled to grasp it so it didn't fall back into the coffee. Pivoting, she slammed it down on the stainless steel prep table across from the roaster and scooped up the trash can by the wall, placing it under the cooling bin shoot. She opened the shoot door and the burnt beans cycled in the cooling bin, spilling into the trash. She crossed her arms over her chest and raised her right hand up to her lips, biting the skin on the side of her thumb nail. Her eyes welled up.

The debris in her coffee beans had been the flash drive recording device that she'd planted in Brent's office.

CHAPTER
TWELVE

Clem stared down at the device in her hand. It wasn't usable, melted on all ends. But she recognized its mangled body by its coloring and the faded, half melted logo on its face.

What were the chances that Brent had found it, known it was hers, and dropped it off here before he'd gone back to his office?

The killer did this. He knew she had been in Brent's office. He knew she'd planted this.

He could have been watching her the entire time. When she was in this building, and everywhere she'd gone in this town. He must have heard her talking to Josie about the recording device back at the restaurant.

He... or... It wasn't proven that it was a he.

Who was everywhere, all the time?

Who had been there the night of Paul's murder?

Who had been in that restaurant when they had dinner and had gone nearly unnoticed?

Who had she run into who had known all about Brent's death?

Polly.

Clementine shuddered. It was the only explanation! She'd trusted Polly. And if Polly was the real murderer, what was she getting at? She had complete access to Clem. Yet, Clem remained unharmed... so far. Perhaps she had been trying to frame her the whole time. But why? What was her motivation for framing Clem? They were friends!

A pounding came from the back room. Clementine nearly leaped out of her skin. She rushed over to the roaster and turned off the agitator, quieting the sound a little. Wide-eyed, she looked around for something, anything that could pose as a weapon. She opted for the closest logical thing, a rubber mallet that she used sometimes to knock the sprocket in the back of the roaster back into place.

The pounding came again.

She slowly walked to the back room, standing in the doorframe and staring down at the floor. The light was off, but late afternoon sunlight came through one of the windows in the office. The floor was spotless concrete. But she had to walk over where Paul's body had lain in a pool of blood not long ago.

Gripping the rubber mallet, she took a deep breath and gathered up the courage.

She marched into the room, staring straight ahead at the door. She wished there was a peephole of any kind. Her only solace was that if this person was here to hurt her, if Polly was here to claim her next victim, then she likely had a key, proven twice now, first with Paul and the now with the fake flash drive. Hell, she probably snatched the building key off of Paul's body. It had never occurred to Clem to ask the police or Simon if the key ring found on Paul was missing the building key, indicating that the killer took it. Why didn't they think about that even? Just another piece of information that proved they could not adequately do their jobs, and that she was on her own.

The pounding again. "Ms. Matthews!"

She stood at attention at the mention of her name in a deep male's voice she did not recognize. "Who's there?" she yelled out, self-conscious for only a moment that her voice shook. She clutched the mallet.

"Roastwood Hollow Fire Department. You called?"

She dropped her arm with the mallet down to her side, heaving a large breath. She reached forward and unlocked the dead bolt, then the knob and pulled it open, revealing one of the firemen from the fire department in full gear. The lights of the truck out front reflected on the building behind the roastery.

"I didn't mean to spook you. You okay?" He asked, his dark eyes genuine.

"OH... this?" She looked down at the mallet. "I was fixing a part of the roaster, no harm done!" She tried to recover, saving face.

"Hi, I'm Dave. I checked your meter out here, and you were right from what dispatch said. Your lines out here were tampered with. Somehow, the threshold was disabled that controlled the flow of gas. That can be really dangerous. You said you were having a problem with your roaster?" He looked around her into the back room.

Her heart beat fast in her chest. Her gas meter had been tampered with. So maybe she *was* intended to be the next victim. Perhaps, after the discovery of the recording device, the killer concluded that she knew too much. "Yeah, I was able to shut off the gas at my line inside, so it stopped from surging into the roaster, where I had the flame ignited. Please come in." She backed up, allowing him to step inside in front of her and charge toward the main room, right over the spot where Paul had lain. Fireman Dave didn't know. "Uh, you probably don't need the truck siren lights on," she said nervously. "I'm just worried I'll have the whole town talking."

He laughed. "It's no worries. I'll walkie them to turn them off. I shouldn't take more than a second to look this over. You did the right thing using your shutoff." He waddled in his heavy gear behind the roaster and poked around, using some meter thing that periodically beeped. As he was back there, she walked over to the prep table and grabbed the melted recording device, pocketing it. Touching the thing sent a shiver up her arm and across the back of her neck.

"Everything seems to be in order now. I would go ahead and put an order in with the gas company to have someone come out and replace your unit."

"So you think someone messed with it? Perhaps someone… was trying to, I don't know, sabotage or hurt me?"

Dave stood to face her with a look of concern, and then typed something into his phone; notes about the visit, she assumed.

"Now I know that something horrific happened here recently. I was sorry to hear about Paul. He was always so kind and kept up with his building permits." His voice sounded very dad-like and concerned. "You've every right to feel uncertain, but you don't need to worry or let paranoia affect your daily life. Sometimes these things just happen with your gas line. Sometimes equipment gets old or malfunctions. That doesn't mean somebody went back there and purposefully messed with your meters to hurt you. There are utility workers checking and messing with meters all the time."

"But it's likely…?" she interjected.

He stared at her for a moment. "I can't say for sure. It didn't look damaged."

"But somebody would need to have a key to open the meter box?"

He nodded slowly. "In most circumstances," he replied quietly. "Ms. Matthews, If you don't feel safe here, perhaps you shouldn't be the only one in here working at a time. The buddy system is always a good rule of thumb. If you've been feeling this way for some time now, I may also recommend you seek extra help to navigate that. "

Was he really recommending a therapist to her? She was impressed. It wasn't often that you heard of first responders putting an emphasis on mental health. Even though she felt mental health was important, and she did speak to a therapist on and off, she didn't feel like this was a matter where she was just paranoid. Then again, this fireman didn't know the details of the whole picture. Or the fact that she just received a message from who she felt was the killer.

"Are you sure you're alright?" he asked, finishing off his notes and pocketing his phone.

She nodded. "Yeah. Thank you for coming out."

He nodded. "Anytime. I'm not doing anything else." They both laughed.

She knew he was making a joke, but in a small town, nothing crazy happened for the fire department apart from a trash can smoking because someone threw their cigarette butt in there. Today, they almost had a whole building fire caused by a roaster that couldn't be calmed down due to a surge in the gas line to the flame. Something someone very much intended to do. She'd been roasting for years and nothing even close to the sort had ever happened. It was definitely intentional.

She walked him to the front door this time instead of the back where the gas lines were and saw him out, waving at the other fireman sitting in the truck, the lights off.

She tucked back inside and shut the door, leaning up against it.

Was she paranoid? Yes.

Was she scared? Yes.

But there was one other very clear emotion that seemed to be taking over her body from head to toe. A fiery rage.

This killer tried to take her out.

A very clear message was received, and she put her hand over the melted lump in her pocket.

They had tried to sabotage her roaster, her livelihood, the foundation of her business. If she hadn't been experienced with the roaster and trained on what to do in a roaster fire, she could have been dead too.

If they didn't want her life, then the message was to back off. And that was one thing that she was very, very, bad at doing. She was all in now.

This meant war.

CHAPTER
THIRTEEN

Clementine rushed into the coffeehouse, Robusta in her harness hanging onto the shoulder of her black hoodie.

"Hello!" A barista called out as she entered the shop, the bells on the door jingling behind her as it slammed. She carried two gallon buckets in her hands, and the barista rushed around the counter to greet her, taking one of the buckets to ease the load.

"Oh hey Clem, more espresso? Thank you, we need this."

She nodded. "Is Josie around?"

"Of course, yeah, she's in the basement. Hey, a bunch of us are doing a D&D campaign over at that one tabletop store in Forestside. Did you want to join?"

"Oh! Uh, when are you having it?"

"I'll text you."

"Cool yeah, thanks. We'll catch up later,
okay?" She set the bucket on the counter and
bolted for the basement. Holding Robusta secure, she peddled down a couple of stairs and
called out into the cellar, "Joes?"

"Yeah! Back here. Inventory."

Clementine finished the stairs and walked
back to the far end, finding Josie with a pencil
in her mouth, holding a clipboard and looking
deep in thought. She pulled the pencil out and
walked up to Clementine, putting a hand on
her arm. "Whoa, you okay? You're white as a
ghost. I mean... you're usually pale, being a
ginger and all, but you're like, *pale* pale."

"No, I am not okay." Clementine reached
into her pocket. She pulled out the melted
recording device and held it out to Josie. "I
didn't know who else to go to."

"What is that—oh, is that the bug?" Her
eyes widened. She set the clipboard down on
top of a case of almond milk and pushed her
curly hair off her shoulder, getting a closer
look at the device. "Did you go back and get
it? What happened to the thing?" She took it
and placed the melted recording device next
to the clipboard.

"You're not going to believe this... I found
it... in the cooling bin of my roaster."

Josie stared at Clementine with her big
eyes, brow furrowed.

"The killer must have found this in Brent's office, and somehow knew I was connected to it. And got a key to my building, and dropped it off to show me they know." Clementine started to pace. Robusta launched off her shoulder onto the deep freeze against the wall, side-eyeing her.

Josie opened her mouth to speak, but Clem cut her off. "I know—I know it sounds insane. It's a stretch, right? But how else did it end up in my roaster?" She fiddled with her hair, twisting it behind her head up into a bun and letting it fall again.

"I don't know…Have you called and told Simon?"

Clem stopped fiddling and wrinkled her nose.

"What? Not speaking to him?"

"Well, for one, he doesn't want me digging into this case anymore. Never did. And I went behind his back and did it anyway, because I had to. And for two, he's probably still mad at me from that dinner." She crossed her arms and leaned back against the backstock syrup shelf.

"I doubt he's angry. He's crazy about you."

"Pshh, What? Come on."

"Everyone sees it but you!"

"Well I've been a little distracted, as you

know. As if I had time for a guy right now anyway. And I did try to call him, but it went straight to voicemail."

Josie laughed. "That's the point. Simon's likely been distracted finding out what happened to Brent. I bet you that's why you haven't heard from him. But anyway, bringing up dinner the other night reminded me of something!"

"Oh?" She stood at attention again, looking to make sure Robusta wasn't getting into trouble. She appeared to just be exploring around the basement.

"Sarah was in here this morning getting a coffee before her shift at The Diner. I asked her why Michael was bussing tables."

"You did *not*," Clem said. "Oh wow, what did she say?"

"It was interesting. She said that he borrowed money from Brent, but couldn't pay it back in time. So he was working shifts to pay off that debt."

Oooh, that was very interesting. "You think... Brent approached Michael like the way he did to me about the building? Only Michael took the deal."

"Sounds like it."

She felt sorry for Michael. She had also experienced Brent's influence, only she didn't let him intimidate her. And if Michael went in on the deal with him, that meant he must have been really desperate. She would have to stop by Michael's boutique soon and see how he was holding up—and also if he'd been approached by the Wright's lawyer or not, given that their buildings had been both owned by Paul.

Speaking of, she needed to reach out to Annette Rhoads, the Wright family's legal rep, and give the news about which path she had decided to take, and see if they would accept it. She'd need to do it soon, before the Snowflake Festival, otherwise she'd get too busy and let it slip away.

"What with Brent gone though, who do you think broke into your roastery?"

Clem bit her bottom lip. "I have a hunch… but it's also going to sound crazy. Believe me."

"Try me."

"I think it might be Polly." Clem whispered, screwing up her face.

"Hm, she does have accessibility. And she does seem to be everywhere. Oh my god, she was there that day at the restaurant! She passed by our table, she probably heard us talking about bugging Brent's office. Remember I was worried about someone eavesdropping?"

Clementine grabbed both of Josie's hands

and gave them a shake. "I *know*, that's exactly what I was thinking!"

"I can't imagine…"

She let go of Josie's hands and spun around, her head in her hands. "…it being her, right!? I mean, she's my *friend*." Her eyes searched for Robusta again, exploring over by the computer desk.

"Okay, okay. Here's what we're going to do. Ryder is upstairs working as a barista right now. He knows computer stuff. He's helped me with setting up all the point-of-sale printers and such. Hang on…" Josie rushed across the basement and picked up the cordless phone on the desk. "Hey, send Ryder down please." She hung up.

Not even a moment later, combat boots hit the stairs.

At the bottom of the steps Ryder looked up at them. In his flannel he looked as though he were embarking on a camping trip instead of a shift behind the bar at Roastwood Coffee. "Am I in trouble?"

Clem laughed into the back of her hand.

"No! Why does everyone think that when I call them down here?" Josie walked over to the almond milk cases and picked up the device, then held it out to him. "Can you take a look at this? Is it usable?"

Ryder squinted, grabbed the device from

Josie, and turned it in his hands. With his head down, he scrutinized Josie, then Clem, then Josie again.

"Are you two doing something illegal?"

They both laughed sheepishly.

"Define… illegal?" Clem's voice rose at the end of the sentence.

"I'm in," Ryder shot back, holding up the device. "I can recover this. Question. Why are you using something from the 1900s? There are so many devices that you could Bluetooth or stream directly to you. Did one of you go and retrieve this?"

Clem tried to keep up. Ryder's Gen-Z was showing hard. 1900's? That was her favorite.

"None of that is relevant, Ryder." Josie crossed her arms.

Clem couldn't help but stifle a laugh again.

"Alright. So the housing of the device is melted, but the insides are intact. Here." He trudged over to the desk and pulled the computer keyboard toward him, reaching behind the modem to plug in the device. "At least your computer still has a USB port. Again, ancient." He eyed Josie.

By now, Clem appreciated his sense of humor. Josie, on the other hand, rolled her eyes before turning to Clem. She spoke softly as Ryder clicked away on the computer. "Are you okay?" She rubbed the side of her arm.

"This could... you know." She lowered her voice. "This could reveal the killer,"

Clem nodded. "I'm ready."

"Okay, it's all good. Just click here and it'll play." Ryder rocked back on his heels.

"Seriously, thank you." Josie heaved toward the computer.

"I think I'll head upstairs before the bar gets backed up. These people need their peppermint mochas."

"Yes, thanks Ryder!" Clem echoed Josie.

He saluted them and headed back up the stairs.

The moment the door shut, Josie clicked the play button.

The entire time they listened to the voices on the device, Clem held her breath. She braced herself with the desk chair, closed her eyes and listened.

One voice.

Then another.

Both familiar.

The voices stopped.

Josie's voice, cracked, interrupted her thoughts, "So what are you going to do about it?"

Clem's chest rose and fell, rattled. "I know what I have to do. I have a plan..."

"If your plan doesn't involve calling the police, then you need a new plan." Josie pointed at her, completely serious. She grabbed her pencil and retrieved her clipboard, then returned to counting the cups and paper products on the shelf.

"I hear you... but anytime I have gone to the police, I don't think they take it seriously. And someone needs to save this town."

Josie continued to look away from Clem, counting the cases of the product. "What, are you Spider-Man now, seeking vigilante justice?"

"I have to try... and I'm going to do it publicly at the Snowflake Festival. If there are lots and lots of witnesses, then I'm safe, right?"

"You would do that... be public with it?"

"Polly killed people, Joes. She set my roaster on fire!"

There was a moment of silence.

Josie dropped the clipboard to her side. "How can I help?"

Clementine smiled and retrieved Robusta, who was heading for the sump pump. "Once I get it organized, I'll text you. Thanks, Josie. You're the best." She went for the stairs.

Josie peered over her shoulder. "Be careful. Don't roast alone right now, okay? And... and you should get a hold of Officer Drake."

Clem nodded. "Heard." Then she turned and ran back up the stairs.

CHAPTER
FOURTEEN

Clementine entered the bank, glancing over to the Christmas tree Brent had her pinned against what seemed like ages ago. She was still reeling over the news she'd discovered down in Roastwood Coffee's basement. But she and Josie had a plan. And that plan required patience. The Snowflake Festival was soon. For now, she needed to take care of some business.

"Greg's been expecting you!" Sandy at the teller window said to her, gesturing her over to his office.

Clem saw another person in there as she approached the door and knocked on the frame. Greg was with Annette, the Wright family's legal representative who she'd met the other day. They both looked up as she entered.

"Welcome in, Clementine," Greg said. "Am I right that you've come to a decision you wanted to discuss with the two of us?" He smiled at her.

"Yes, uh, Ms. Rhoads. Thank you for coming down here. I've gotten my affairs in order where it comes to the building on Oak Street? Paul's building." She stopped to take a breath, nerves getting the best of her. "I wanted to get you this right away, as I'm sure Paul's family wants to get this settled as quickly as possible."

"That's very considerate of you, yes." Annette sat down in one of the arm chairs across from Greg, the banker. She gestured to Clem to do the same next to her.

Clem moved around the chair and sat parallel to the pant-suited executor, remaining at the edge of the armchair.

"Right. So we ran my financial profile here at the bank, and I've been informed—correct me if I'm wrong, Greg—but I qualify for a loan that will allow me to buy the building outright from the Wright's. I definitely want the building. I worried whether I could qualify or have enough funds to buy it outright. If I didn't, I would have gone for the rent-to-own option. However, Greg tells me that the bank is willing to host a loan for me here."

Greg nodded. "Roastwood Coffee is really important to our community, and none of us want to see you out of a building, Clem. We know you are good for it, and we are here to support you, financially or otherwise."

Her chest warmed, and she couldn't help but smile. Her cheeks felt flushed. She knew that she stayed in this small town for a reason. And yes, she complained about the catty-ness and the cliques in Roastwood Hollow, and that privacy was hard to come by. However, there were pros to this small river town too, and here was one of them staring her right in the face.

"Of course I'm relieved and grateful for the Wright family's willingness to work with me, however I honestly just wish Paul was still here. Since he's not, I want to do that building justice and I want to keep what we had going."

Annette nodded, smiling. "And that's why they've offered this opportunity. I have the paperwork drawn up here, done in advance just in case. And Greg here is a notary for the bank, so two birds with one stone. Once you sign these papers, it's yours. You already have a key. And Greg will finish out the loan paperwork and money transfer to the Wright's."

She pulled the paperwork out of her bag in a manila folder and opened it on the desk.

"Here you are! Sign here, here, and here."

Greg leaned forward over his desk with a pen for her.

Clementine retrieved it and thanked him, then leaned over and scanned the paperwork. Everything seemed to be in order with all that they discussed. She signed and dated the bottom of each paper, the metal pen cool between her fingers, then pushed it back towards Annette.

"That's it then?" she asked.

"That's it." Annette closed the folder. "Congratulations, Ms. Matthews."

Clem smiled, a huge wave of relief washing over her. Obviously, it wasn't and would never be an easy road. She'd now have a mortgage and property taxes to worry about on that building. But it wasn't any different than paying rent and utilities and getting no investment in return. This situation was the best decision for her and her business.

And not only that, but with signing on the dotted line, she was finally able to feel some resolution. Resolution of the worries about the fate of her business, at least.

Paul had done this for her, even in death. That meant she needed to repay him by bringing his killer to justice.

CHAPTER
FIFTEEN

Clementine's reflection stared back at her in the mirror. Striking orange waves framed the sides of her face. Her green eyes pierced in the dim light, accentuated by the dark mascara she'd applied that morning. She wore a black t-shirt bearing Roastwood Coffee's logo, a mug with illustrated latte art in the cup. And black skinny jeans. A hunter green sweater cardigan shielded the many sunny tattoos that blanketed her arms.

Today was a big day. The Snowflake Festival. The event that had consumed Roastwood Hollow's townsfolk and small business owners since August, when their end of summer festival ended. The Snowflake Festival had been going on for more than twenty years, and marked the start of the holiday season and winter for Roastwood Hollow. It took place in the evening, after a lot of the businesses closed. Josie always kept Roast-wood Coffee open late to provide guests with ciders and hot chocolates while they watched the children choir in the park.

Clem needed to make sure she had enough coffee beans to host the extended hours. She left the bathroom and entered the main area of the roastery. The Snowflake Festival would be wildly different this year, mainly due to her plan to publicly out a household name. She sighed and took a look around.

A quiet moment. The ambient sound of the furnace humming gave her solace. It was all hers, no barriers: the business, and now the building as well. It was as though something had changed overnight. Nothing physical had, but everything internally had. It was a feeling like she'd never quite felt before. Ful-fillment. Joy.

However, the underlying uneasiness couldn't be ignored. It was partly because she told a lot of people she wouldn't be in this building alone: Josie...fireman Dave... Simon. Yet here she was, alone in the roastery. She had this feeling of calm before the storm; that after this moment, everything was going to change.

And as to her being in here alone, she didn't like the idea of anyone ruling her life.

In the face of danger, Clem almost saw it as a challenge to continue to do what was convenient for her. To alter her schedule or uproot someone else's day for the buddy system, felt like she'd already lost. If Polly wanted to come here and try to put an end to her, Clem would be ready. After she prepared the coffee for the festival today, she would meet Josie down at the park and set up their table where they would be selling and serving together. So she got straight to work, filling a few buckets with the special Snowflake Blend she'd created, as well as the pitchers of cold brew she prepped yesterday. No matter how cold it was, the people wanted a cold brew coffee.

She packed all the buckets and pitchers into a collapsible wagon outside the front door to the roastery, then ducked back inside to turn the lights off. She locked the door behind her and started the journey towards the park by the river. As she walked, she ran all the details over in her head again.

Polly was watching from afar the night she called the police about Paul. Polly heard her in the diner talk about putting the recording device in Brent's office. So she went in after Clem left and retrieved it, then killed Brent, then planted it in the roastery. She must have snatched the key to the roastery off Paul's body before leaving that night.

Polly knew everyone and everything about everyone. She wasn't shy about sharing information. She was a trusted community member. She had a knack for making everyone feel like they were special, that they were the only ones she was sharing that information with—until word got around.

And it always did.

It was highly suspicious that whenever the deaths were mentioned, in the community meeting after Paul died and in the conversation she had with Polly *right* after she'd found out about Brent's demise, Polly was quick to change the subject, and seemed all together unconcerned.

All of this was enough for Clementine to feel like Polly was the one.

And then… Polly's voice on the recording device.

There was only one problem. As she pulled the wagon of supplies down the sidewalk, waiting for passing cars before crossing the street, and then dragging it over the bumps of the train tracks into the park, she could not for the life of her think what Polly's motive would be with any of the killings. She was just going to have to blatantly ask her. And very publicly…

Most of the time, the motive wasn't entirely clear until someone was caught anyway.

At least, that's what she'd learned from movies and crime podcasts. And more importantly, she knew that members of the police force were going to be present at the festival. She wasn't sure about Simon, since they weren't really talking, but chances were high that he was going to be there. Her chest tightened at the thought. She hadn't made amends with him yet like Josie had recommended. And the more time that passed, the harder it became.

CHAPTER
SIXTEEN

S nowflake banners marked the main street, and planters with festive holly and red berries lined the walk. All of the buildings had large light bulbs lining their trim, illuminating the whole town and leading all the way into the park on the river.

She rounded the corner into the park, immediately regretting the choice of a wagon. "Why didn't I just drive down here?" she questioned as she saw other vendor's trucks pulling into the park and unloading. She figured since her shop was so close, a wagon would be good enough. But the terrain wasn't flat and the cold brew was sloshing around in the pitchers, especially when she'd hit even the slightest rock.

"Oh, let me give you a hand with that!"

Clementine's head jerked up to see Polly, as jolly as could be in her red fuzzy sweater and dangling candy cane earrings, coming straight towards her. Clementine recoiled. "No! No, it's okay, I got it."

Polly laughed. "Are you sure? You look like you could use a hand, sweetie."

"Mmm no, Josie is right down there with the other vendors. I'm meeting her. It's fine. Thanks though, I got it." She tried to avoid eye contact as she walked right past Polly. That might have been a mistake. She was supposed to be acting like nothing out of the ordinary was going on, not raising any alarms that she suspected Polly was the killer. She couldn't tip her off.

"Well alright! I'll go check and see if the Boy Scouts got Santa's house in the right location. But you let me know if you need any help. The fire department will be around soon to do booth inspections."

She was in full swing festival mode. She had such a good cover. Such a good alibi. It made her even more suspicious.

Clementine refocused on finding Josie down the line of vendors. She waved at Michael as she passed his booth, folding hipster style shirts on his tables. "I'll be by for coffee later!," he said. "I need something hot. It's colder out here than normal."

"I got you!" she shouted at him, continuing to walk.

She passed the quilting ladies, organizing some red and green holiday-themed quilts onto ladders as shelves. She put her hand up to wave, but those ladies never really seemed to like her, so she put her hand back down, hoping they didn't notice her rolling by. She wasn't sure what they had against her, except maybe she'd parked in their parking spot a time or two. They were never shy about leaving a note on her windshield. This being a small town and all, there was no denying that it wasn't her car. She'd try to make it up to them by dropping off their favorite drinks, but that didn't even matter. They remained grumpy.

Alas, she had more important things to worry about.

"Clem! It took you long enough." Josie teased as she rounded the table and took the wagon handle from her, pulling it behind the booth. "The fire marshal is going to be here soon for inspection. We have the third slot in line."

Clementine nodded and ducked under the table to get behind the booth. She looked out at all the other vendors setting up. The park was marked with tables and tent booths, rounding into a large circle with a stage at the top. It looked from above as though it were a large ornament, with the stage being the hanger.

"So you brought beans and cold brew?"

Clementine snapped out of it, helping Josie unload the wagon. She turned to check out the setup Josie had for the espresso bar and grinder. "This is pretty neat." Clementine grabbed a bucket of the espresso beans from the wagon and loaded the grinder, the beans clinking into the hopper, then stored the bucket underneath the table. "You got every-thing you need here?" It was a rhetorical question, because of course she knew Josie would have everything she needed, and prob-ably extra. Clementine continued to fidget with the cups.

"Mmm, that espresso smells so good."

"Good, some of the beans are a little older, from last week." Clementine sidled over to Josie, a whiff of the bin wafting over to her. "I haven't had much opportunity the last few days to roast new batches."

"You seem… distracted?" Josie pointed out.

Clementine laughed under her breath. "Yeah, you could say that."

"You thinking about your plan?" she asked.

Clem looked back and forth, then looked Josie in the eyes and nodded.

"Good afternoon, ladies!" The fire marshal approached their booth, clipboard to his broad chest. "Permit?"

"Yes, absolutely! Clem, hand me the binder on top of that tote there."

Clementine shuffled, looking at the tote under the table in front of her, a gray binder on top. She snatched it and handed it to Josie, who pulled out a few papers and handed them to the marshal.

"No generator?"

Josie shook her head. Clem was glad that Josie took care of all this. She was too distracted and had too many other things to think about. They'd done this festival and many others together for years. They just sort of got into a groove. Usually they would both have other staff work them, but the Snowflake Festival was the most important one of the year for the town. They couldn't miss it.

"Handwashing station?"

Josie showed him over to the cooler of water she had situated behind them, spilling into an empty bucket below. Soap next to it, and paper towels hanging from a bungee cord connected to the tent: requirements of the health inspectors, which would likely be by next and the Fire Marshal was trying to speed things along.

"Looks great, let me know if there's anything you need from us as the festival goes on. We're on standby."

"Thank you, Marshal Daniels. We will." Josie reinstated the paperwork into the binder and stashed it below again.

Just as the marshal was walking away, Clem called out to him, "Marshal Daniels! What other first responders do we have available for the festival tonight?"

"Well… we have a security guard in the parking lot, a few volunteers helping park cars, and there is a small group of officers at the check-in station just over there," he pointed across the circle diagonally from them, "you know, for assistance with lost kids and such."

And to arrest murderers… she thought quickly.

"Fingers crossed they don't have much activity tonight!" he boomed cheerfully, then moved onto the next tent.

"Well done, Josie." Clem said, patting her on the shoulder. Josie chuckled, knowing full well that Clem wanted nothing to do with that part. The mutual agreement was that if she had to step up, she most definitely would.

Clem's gaze followed the path the fire marshal pointed out to the check-in tent where the officers would be stationed. It was hard to tell from far away, but she strained her eyes, catching a glimpse of one of the officers as he turned laughing into the air.

It was him. *Simon.* The way he seemed happy made her chest warm. She had been such a jerk to him. She would make amends. It was this whole matter of the bigger picture. She wanted to make amends and hang out with him and get to know him better, but there was a literal killer on the loose. Now maybe it was true that they had more puzzle pieces than her, but she couldn't sit back and do nothing. Perhaps that tenacity would lose her getting to know this really great person. She'd already tried to get a hold of him once, and he hadn't returned her call. Reaching out went both ways.

"Why don't you just go talk to him already?" Josie pushed, as though she could read her mind. Or maybe it was her questions to the fire marshal and the intense staring that gave it away.

"I will…" Clem breathed.

"You have time right now, before everything gets going. I mean, the kids choir is just starting to arrive, and you know that's when all their parents get here. They're bussing kids in, did you see it?"

Clem's heart began to race. She brushed her clammy hands on her thighs. What was that all about? Anticipation for the festival?

For catching the killer? For … Simon? *No way.* Not here and not now.

Things were finally starting to pick up. She welcomed the distraction. Michael stopped by the table and got his coffee to take back to his boutique tent, as promised. Townsfolk and out-of-towners were let into the park through registration. The event itself was free to the public, they just liked to track how many guests came and went.

The park grounds felt way more breathable since they didn't have the carnival set up this time. In the aftermath of Paul's murder, when she'd stayed home, the town must have agreed not to bring the carnival back this year. And she was happy about that. Something about carnivals really creeped her out. She didn't like the idea of entertainment and thrill rides being folded up and carted around on trailer trucks. Surely the quality control on those couldn't be great. Also, throughout the years, the people that ran the carnival would come into the coffee shop, and they were strange folks: up early, out late at night, never liked to be in one spot for too long.

Not to mention the carnival took up so much space in the town, mostly where they had city parking, which made the downtown area very congested. She knew they'd be back for the next festival, but she got a little break for this year.

She snapped out of her thoughts as Josie put down two cups on the bar. Clem picked them up and read the drink codes she'd written. Two cold brews. She poured from the pitcher and topped the cups with ice, then lidded them and handed them off. Helping customers truly quickened the time. Soon enough the river park grounds were full of people.

The entertainment on the stage was in full swing. A local folk band started with a traditional Christmas set of songs to get things warmed up. She looked at the stage which was fully equipped with the sound system and lighting. They had volunteers run it during the festival. It was quite an impressive setup for a small town, but churches and schools used the outdoor stage during the off seasons. Roastwood Hollow had spent tons of money on the stage's renovation after not one, but two semi-trucks plowed into the pavilion, which set off an insurance battle to see who had to pay out. Once a settlement was reached with the insurance companies of the two truck companies, and after receiving a grant from the city, they were able to rebuild the stage for communal use and make it much more functional. Of course, not without all the opinions of people who felt they should be the ones to make decisions on behalf of the town.

Clem's stomach lurched into her throat when she spotted Polly, running back and forth, assisting where she could. Part of her felt guilty, knowing what was coming on that stage. Polly seemed to work so hard on this festival. It occurred to Clem that it might be in her best interest to do it sooner and not give Polly more time to commit another crime. Her cover was the best; as Clem had heard before, the best place to hide was in plain sight. And Polly was certainly front and center.

Clem also had nerves so bad that her stomach hurt. She was never one to draw attention to herself. She liked to be in the background of situations. She was the observer, not the perpetrator. But today was going to be different. She had to come out of her shell and just do it, for the sake of everyone in this town.

The folk group finished up, with several claps in the audience and a large mass of children took the stage, guided by several teachers. Clem smiled at the couple that approached the table, motioning them toward Josie to take the order.

"What a great idea for this festival! I'll take a coffee and two hot chocolates." Josie wrote up the cups and set them down. Clem grabbed them, getting to work.

She finished them up and set them on the table. "Hey Josie, I'm going to go talk to the sound guy, I'll be right back. I need to get prepared."

"You okay?"

"Yeah, just nervous. This is a big deal."

Josie scoffed. "Yeah it is. Have you seen how busy she is?"

"Yeah, I see her," Clem said. Josie looked longingly into the crowd.

"Believe me, I wish it was someone else. But if Polly is responsible…" she whispered, "then she did some pretty messed up stuff, Joes. The families need justice." That was beginning to fire her up. And there was still what she held in her pocket. Did Polly think the recording device was going to be damaged when she dropped it back off?

Or… or maybe it wasn't Polly that brought it back to her, after all. Maybe someone was trying to get the information to her that it *was* Polly. Now her mind was starting to spiral.

Why would the actual killer return concrete evidence, unless she was certain that the device was damaged and there was no chance of anyone hearing the recording? Just to scare Clem off, like a small wink to her that the killer knew she had bugged Brent's office?

Josie tapped her leg. "And you're sure they both weren't just… well, death by suicide and heart attack?" Josie pumped some chocolate sauce into a cup. "This town doesn't want the negative publicity. Just think, would all these people be here right now if they knew that there was a killer on the loose?"

"Hello Roastwood Hollow!" A booming voice came over the PA system as the cheery Christmas music sung by the kids faded out. Diane from the Main Street Association was emceeing the event, as she always did. Usually, Clementine would tune her out. This time she listened, because this was the start of her plan.

By now, the event grounds were hopping. "Next, who can tell me what Frosty the Snowman says when he wakes up using the magic top hat?"

Kids shouted in the crowd.

"Yes! He says 'happy birthday.' You there in the green shirt, come up and pull a gift card out of the basket. All of our wonderful shops donated gift cards for you to win."

Clem stood with her hand on her hip, her other hand to her mouth, chewing on a fingernail.

"We're going to get our next group up here in just a second, but please enjoy this Christmas music recording from one of our own, The Green Sleeves Band." Diane put the microphone onto the stand and moved off the stage.

Just when Clementine reached to help Josie with another drink, it was happening.

The Green Sleeves Band's music started, but abruptly stopped. Then, out of the PA speakers for the entire town to hear came static, as though something was rubbing the microphone, followed by a clear conversation between the distinct voices of Brent, and none other than Polly.

Clem quickly glanced uncomfortably over to Josie. The two of them had heard this recording before. Josie stood rigid, wide-eyed. "Your plan was to play this for everyone to hear?" she pressed through gritted teeth.

Clem nodded quickly, her brow carrying lines of worry as she backed away from the bar and glazed over to the stage, then continued to chew her nail.

"You really are a pain in my side, you know that?" The woman's voice continued in the conversation.

"I have to be, Polly, it's in my blood." Brent's cocky and confident voice boomed over the speakers.

"You better watch your back, that's all I'm saying."

Clementine broke her concentration to

watch the chaos that ensued in the center of the grounds of vendor tents. Gasps erupted from the crowd, all looking around and scrambling until they locked eyes on Polly, the executive director: the person everyone knew and that knew everyone.

Diane frantically argued into her Bluetooth headset, then headed for the back of the crowd where the sound booth controlled the PA system. Then she stopped to listen to the recording, something that was clearly *not* supposed to be in the program, and froze, eyes wide.

"Just take the settlement and keep your mouth shut," Brent said, his tone changed. It was dark, threatening. Everyone in that crowd knew how his story ended.

"There's not enough money in the world you could give me…" That was enough to set the wheels in motion. Polly was panicking in plain sight. She dropped the clipboards of the itinerary and notes she was holding and even her phone. The police in the station right next to hers at registration were surrounding her. She held her hands up in surrender.

"I mean, sure, yes, I said those things, but I didn't KILL him! Is that what this is about? C'mon guys, you know me," she shouted to the crowd, raised her hands, and shook them in front of her.

The three officers moved in. "C'mon Polly, don't make this harder than it has to be. This doesn't have to be a scene. Clearly someone has some incriminating evidence on you. And Brent is dead. We at least need your statement."

"Why do you need those for a statement?" She pointed to the handcuffs that Simon had retrieved from his belt.

Clem held her breath.

"Just a precaution." He shrugged, looking to the other cops for approval, which they gave. "We can do the Miranda rights in private, okay?"

Suddenly Clementine felt very uncomfortable, as though she was witnessing something intimate. People had their phones out. The recording had been turned off, but they'd heard enough.

"This is ridiculous! Who even... how did anyone get that recording? Isn't it illegal to record someone without their consent?"

"There are a few other things more incriminating in this situation than that, Polly," one of the other cops said.

"But I didn't—"

"They all say that. Now let's go."

"Hands behind your back, please." Simon did his job. He gently grabbed her wrists and bound them, crimping each cuff together, then guided Polly back up to the parking lot.

"All right, folks! That was… unexpected and clearly not part of the programing. I'm sure we will get more information after the good people of law enforcement sort things out. Surely they'll work it out." Diane's bubbly voice through the loudspeaker tried to get the attention of the crowd back on the festival.

"Now, lots of folks have worked really hard on this festival tonight. We'd like to thank our partners for their donations, and there will be a wonderful fireworks display starting at eight pm, so please stick around. Coming up next is the local children's choir from Roastwood and Forestside elementary schools."

The kids were ushered in at an astronomical pace, and quicker than everything had happened, it was back to normal again with the events of the festival.

Karma. It wasn't any different than that community meeting. When the police gave a tiny piece of important information, but not the whole picture, the community brushed it under the rug and continued to plan this festival as though it were more important. Clem was really whiplashed by the priorities. Did they not think those things were important, or were they just trying to distract from the tragedy?

For the first time, Clementine stopped to think about Simon's feelings in the whole thing. There was no way that Polly or Simon knew that Clem was behind getting that recording to the PA system volunteers. And a small amount of anger surfaced, because Polly was the one that returned that recording in the first place. Of course, she wasn't smart enough to know that it wasn't damaged beyond retrieval, it had only been cosmetically damaged. And evidently Polly didn't think anything got put on that recording. She seemed pretty good at acting as though she had no idea what was going on. It almost seemed… genuine.

A hand landed on Clem's shoulder. She quickly glanced over at Josie.

"You okay?"

Clem let out a long breath. "I don't think I breathed during that entire thing."

"You need to sit down." Josie yanked a milk crate from under the table and flipped it upside down in the grass. "Here."

Clem slumped down onto the milk crate, putting her head in her hands for a moment and rubbing her head. "Well, I *want* to feel relief… but I just, I don't know. Paul and Brent's deaths deserve to be put to justice. I just still don't want to believe that it was Polly, you know?"

Josie tapped her back again. "It'll get worked out, okay? You did the right thing."

"Did I?"

"Yes! And now the right thing for you to do is get up here with me and sling this darn good coffee out to our community. Your hard work deserves to be consumed and enjoyed. And you deserve to serve it without feeling like you're next."

Clem smirked at Josie, the one who was always calm under pressure and always knew the right thing to say. She stood back up and went to the makeshift handwashing station.

"But first… " Josie handed her a coffee cup.

"It's okay, I don't need caffeine this late—"

"Drink it."

Clem laughed. "Fine. I guess I could use something warm." She brought it to her lips, the unexpected flavor and burn in her throat hitting her, her eyes wide. "Whoa." Not the kind of warmth she expected.

"Whiskey," Josie said under her breath.

Clementine laughed again. "When did you stash this?" she asked, taking another sip. "You know what, nevermind. I need this, you're right. Just don't mistake these cups for what you give the customers."

Josie laughed. "Clementine Matthews, what do you take me for?"

Clem shook her head. This evening was heavy. And far more on the agenda than she originally planned for the annual Snowflake Festival. But because of what she did, maybe, just maybe, she would finally get to sleep tonight without the thought that there was a murderer on the loose, and without the fear that she was next.

CHAPTER
SEVENTEEN

L ife took a turn in the following days. It was almost easy again. Clementine didn't have to look over her shoulder when she got out of her car at the roastery. Robusta joined her again and they worked in peace. Lo-fi beats blasted over her soundbar and the roaster cooked up more batches of beans than she had in over a week. She cruised back and forth between her order notes and measuring out the beans to fulfill them. Though she was productive, she couldn't help but think back to that evening under the colors of the fireworks bursting in the sky.

This year's fireworks at the Snowflake Festival were bittersweet. They finished off a Roastwood Hollow tradition primarily organized by the same person who had been taken away to jail right in front of them. Conflicting thoughts and emotions surrounded the ordeal, and it was a lot to unpack. Perhaps she'd even go and visit Polly in the jail to ask her questions for some sort of closure. There hadn't been a clear motive like she'd hoped. Clem had imagined the plot unraveling in front of her at the Snowflake Festival like a movie: like Scooby-Doo unmasking the villain. Only... that sort of closure had not happened. The whole thing was off.

She also needed to repair the relationship she'd only just begun with Simon, even if the endgame was friendship. He was a nice guy. And she admitted to herself that she had been a little childish with their interaction. He had told her to lay off the case, and she didn't listen and kept going anyway. How did he feel about that now, having caught the killer? Simon didn't know that Clem had provided the recording. And she was happy keeping that anonymous, considering how Polly had yelled out in defense as she was taken away.

It wasn't entirely legal to record someone without their consent. Clem didn't want to blow herself in that she was the one who planted the device, and then orchestrated its reveal at the festival. But... but Polly must have known it was her. And that hurt considering their friendship. Because now Polly knew that Clem knew, and it had been several days since the arrest, but no cops had come for her. Which meant Polly hadn't told them that she'd dropped that device off at the roastery. If Polly was already in trouble, why not take another down with her? It was interesting, to say the least.

Clem set the container on a chair up against the cooling bin of the roaster, pulling the lever for the beans to spill into it. They had cooled enough to be stored, and she checked that the gas was off to begin cooling down the roaster for the day. She stood back and looked at her work. Feeling quite accomplished, she walked over to the sitting area and picked up her gray sweater cardigan, throwing it over her shoulders with her arms into the sleeves. She picked Robusta up; the reptile wore a turquoise crocheted sweater, a perfect fit. Clem held Ro to her chest and stroked her head. Then she picked the harness and leash up off a nearby stack of pallets and clipped it on Ro. "What do you say we go get a snack?"

She carried Robusta over to the roaster and powered it down, since it had gotten under two hundred degrees. Then she turned off the lights to the roastery and left out the door, locking it behind her.

On a day like today, the walk felt much longer with a brisk breeze stinging her cheeks. She held Robusta close, who did not fare well in cold weather. The bearded dragon would have much preferred to be underneath a heating lamp. Clem tucked Ro into her cardigan to keep her shaded from the harsh wind that nipped her nose.

They rounded the corner, and Clem caught the door as a customer left out of it.

It was nearing closing time, and the place was pretty empty. The two baristas looked up at the door in unison at the ringing bell. Their expressions held crushed hopes of an early night, thanks to another customer so close to closing time.

"Just me!" Clem put her free hand up in surrender as she approached the register. She laughed, knowing how they felt, having served many years as a barista at this very cafe. "Well… and Ro," she added.

"Robusta! You haven't brought her here in a while! Can I?" The barista with a blond bob excitedly circled around the counter and propped a broom and dustpan against the wall to take Robusta from Clem.

"Of course." She handed her over, and Robusta's legs swam in the air a moment before she could claw onto the shoulder of the barista.

"You want something before I put up the beans?" Ryder asked from behind the counter.

"Uhh yeah, do you guys have eggnog yet?"

"Do. We. Have. Eggnog," he repeated, side-eyeing her.

She laughed. "Okay, I guess you've been making a lot of those then! Well I will also have one, because they are delicious. Eggnog latte please, just a small one."

"You got it." The barista said happily and the whirl of the grinder revved up.

"Hey you." Josie rounded the corner, coming out of the back.

"Hey. How's it been going around here?"

Josie walked behind the counter and opened up the register with a key. "Busy. Well, you know with the amount of orders we just put in." She faced the bills inside, prepping the drawer to count and close it out.

"Yeah! I'll have those over soon. I got a lot done today. I just came over after I finished for a snack. Thought I'd catch you."

"Eggnog latte?" She glanced over at the counter where the barista was steaming the milk, the steam wand screaming in the pitcher.

Clem laughed. "Of course!"

"You know who was just in here?"

"Who?"

"Officer Drake," Josie sang, then counted the bills.

"Why would I need to know that?" Clem stood her ground, looking over at the barista loving on Robusta. Robusta loved it right back.

"You need to mend things." She cocked her eyebrow at Clem like an older sister.

"I will. I know."

"Here you go, Clem!" Ryder put the eggnog latte on the counter and slid it to her. Clementine picked it up and sipped from the lid hole. She closed her eyes as the warmth went down her throat. So festive. So creamy. So sweet. Just what she needed to end the productive workday.

"Oh hey, I almost forgot. Michael over at Made in The Hollow said he needed to talk to you, and to send you his way."

"Oh?"

"It was something about wanting to do a custom blend for a pop-up he's having soon. He was in here earlier grabbing a coffee and wanted me to pass on the information."

Clem took another sip. "You don't think he's still over there, do you? Don't they close earlier than us?"

"He was saying they stay open late for the holidays. He should still be over there, most likely. But you might want to get it cleared up before you forget." Josie laughed, then looked down and started to count the next stack of bills.

"Well okay, you think you could keep Robusta till I get back? It's chilly out there, and I'm sure she'd like it a lot more than coming with me."

"Uhm, yes, seriously anytime."

"Great! I shouldn't be too long. Lock me out?"

She headed for the door, her coffee cup in hand.

"Right behind ya." Ryder followed her to the door. She opened it and waved, hearing him lock it behind her. She felt in her back pocket for her phone and took another sip of her hot latte, which felt amazing going down her throat in the cold, crisp air.

CHAPTER
EIGHTEEN

Michael's boutique lights were still on across the street. She looked both ways and then crossed, jumping up on the sidewalk and approaching the door. She pulled open the door and a dainty bell dinged. She looked around the little boutique, sipping her eggnog. Local goods, shirts, candles, beauty care products, tote bags, and more. The shirts were all designed by local graphic designers, sporting trendy designs popular in the coffee industry as well. She was going to have to come back when she had more time to do some Christmas shopping.

Another customer was across the way, shopping the men's cologne and aftershave section.

"Clementine!" Michael called as he came out from the back room of the boutique. He nodded and smiled at the other customer as he approached her.

"Hi! Josie said you wanted to discuss something with me?"

"Yes! You do custom coffee blends, right?" He went over to the register and walked behind it, fidgeting with things on the counter.

Clem followed him over. "Yes, of course!"

"I wanted to talk about it at the Snowflake Festival, but then we both saw—" he leaned in and cupped his palm to his mouth, as if sharing a secret, "—THAT went down."

Clementine nodded. It wasn't one of those inner circle things she could chuckle at—not these circumstances. "Yeah. I'd love to help you curate something. What were you thinking?"

"Well we are going to be doing a pop-up sip and shop for holiday shoppers, and instead of doing spiked drinks, I thought maybe we could do coffee?"

"Ooo, a sip and shop, sign me up!" The shopper came up to the counter with a pile of goods in her hands. Clementine smiled and stepped away from the counter for her to check out.

"I'll have up my fliers for it Janet, you won't miss it!" Michael smiled as he removed hangers and folded shirts, ringing them up on the table.

"Hey, I'll let you get back to your work, and we can catch up about your custom blend later! I'd love to do one with you." Clementine turned on her heels to head back to the coffeehouse.

"No! Clem, wait." There was a tone in his voice. She looked over her shoulder.

"46.82, Janet, thank you so much." He moved the folded shirts and soaps into a handled paper bag as Janet swiped her card.

"Just hold on a moment longer. There was something I wanted to show you real quick before you go." He told Clem as he finished up the transaction.

Clem shrugged and moved to the window to check out the football inspired Christmas tree in the window.

"Thank you so much for shopping small!" He said to Janet as she thanked him and grabbed her bag. She headed for the door, smiling at Clem on the way out. Clem watched Michael follow behind Janet and wave goodbye at the door. When she'd completely left, he pulled the door closed and slid his key into the slot, locking it and pocketing his keys once more.

"Oh, you're closing up? Josie said you—"

"Yeah, we've been slow. I wanted to show you something in my basement."

"Okay? Yeah... I have a minute or so..."

She followed him towards the back. "I have my beardy with me,so I can't be gone from the coffeehouse for too long."

He approached the door, shoulders hunched.

"I didn't know that you had a finished cellar like the coffeehouse."

He creaked open the door, the basement dark. "After you." He gestured his hand.

"Oh? It's dark…"

"The light's at the bottom."

Everything about this told her to leave. She didn't have a good feeling about going into this dark basement, and Michael was acting weird. But it was Michael. What was there to worry about?

She held onto the railing and placed one foot in front of the other, walking down into the dark basement. A musty smell filled her nose as she went further down. The light from upstairs disappeared as Michael closed the basement door behind them.

Clem heard a click behind her. Did Michael lock the door?

"What is going on, Michael?"

"Just a few more stairs…" His voice was low and quiet.

She kept walking.

"Did you lock it?" Just as she was about to stop and run back up the stairs, she felt a big shove from behind. She fell forward, tumbling down the last few stairs and hitting the ground hard with an *oomph*. It was definitely just earth, not cement.

Instinctually she fumbled for her phone in her back pocket, but to her dismay, it was not there. She choked on the musty air as foot-steps menacingly thumped down the stairs, one by one.

She pushed back on the dirt a little bit, but didn't want to go too far because she couldn't see her surroundings. "Michael!" she shouted again, still in disbelief at what was happening.

There was silence for a moment. No more feet on the stairs.

Then, a burst of light with a clink.

When her eyes adjusted, Michael stood be-tween her and the stairs. Only it wasn't Michael. His eyes were different. They weren't kind and goofy and friendly and neighborly. They were targeted and vengeful and calcu-lated. It was like something was possessing the Michael she knew. Only, did she really even know who Michael was to begin with? She *thought* she did.

She eyed her phone by his feet. It had slipped out of her back pocket when she hit the floor. Dang girl jeans and their short, worthless pockets. She tried not to draw attention to it. Maybe she could find an opportunity to reach forward and grab it.

As soon as she thought about it, he looked down. He smirked, then kicked the phone across the floor. She heard it hit against the stone wall to her right.

Now that she'd gotten a good look at her surroundings, it was definitely an unfinished basement. It didn't have standard sized ceilings like the coffeehouse basement did. She certainly wouldn't put anything down here if it was in her building. It was musty, damp, and small. Very small.

"You've caused me a lot of problems." His voice was low and accusatory.

"Excuse me?" she batted back.

"Hands behind your back."

She opened her mouth to argue when he cut her off.

"No speaking!"

She shook at the harshness of it, and put her hands behind her.

"Now turn around!"

"I'm on the gro—"

"Now."

She used her feet out in front of her to rotate on the floor, creating a small dust cloud of dirt, facing her back to him. She heard shuffling as he yanked both her wrists. A hard bit of plastic brushed her wrist, then she heard the zip as he pulled the strap tight. Zip ties. That's why they called them that. Thoughts ran through her mind at a million miles a second, but at the same time she was frozen, trying to piece things together. Nothing made sense. Why was he doing this? How had she caused *Michael* a lot of problems?

He jerked her around to face him again. "Then again... you also *helped* me at the Snowflake Festival."

What did he mean? By providing coffee? "By... by offering a custom blend for your pop-up?" she asked timidly.

"No, you idiot, I only said that as a cover to get you to come over here."

She scoffed. "Well, it worked."

"Clearly!" He started to pace in front of her.

It made her more nervous to watch him act nervously. She scanned him. He didn't seem to have any weapons on him, no guns, or knives. This looked like, perhaps, he wasn't prepared to kidnap her. Maybe he wasn't expecting her to return his call so quickly and he panicked, thinking there wouldn't be another opportunity. What had Clementine Matthews helped him with at the Snowflake Festival, if it had nothing to do with coffee?

Something big.

Something like Polly's arrest.

Clem's heart beat harder in her chest, her mouth dry, her stomach swirling with nerves. She took a stab in the dark. "Why did you wait for me to come here... when you have a key to the roastery?"

"Because every time I go over there, you're —" He paused.

Busted. Only, this wasn't the news she hoped for, because that meant she was trapped in a basement cellar with none other than...

"Clever," he concluded. "But you weren't clever enough to learn that before now."

She dropped her head, letting out an exasperated sigh, the first time she'd breathed in minutes, it felt like. "You don't want to do this, Michael."

"Oh, I really think I do." He reached in his pocket and pulled out a glass container the size of his pinkie finger, small enough to disguise. "Enough of this will put you out, then I can do as I please."

Her heart raced. She didn't know what was in that tube, but she knew it was dangerous. "Is that..." *Just keep him talking, Clem.* The Michael she had known loved to talk. *Just keep him talking.* "Is that how you made Paul's death look like a suicide?"

Silence. But Michael looked down at the

vial and then at her. "You're not as dumb as you look."

She barely heard the words enough to be insulted. "But then… how did you make Brent's appear like a heart attack?"

More silence. She hated the silences. She didn't know what he was thinking. She didn't want to give him time to think. She was about to speak again when he responded, "It presents and interacts with people in different ways."

She knew it. Why had she never thought of Michael as a suspect? He was that good at having alibis. A pinch of emotion gripped her at the realization that she'd thought it was Polly for even a second. Polly's arrest had never felt like a conclusion without knowing *why*. So she thought she'd try to find out. "Why though, Michael?" She wracked her brain. "You were bussing tables at Brent's diner. Did you… did you borrow money you couldn't repay? Did he own you?"

"You shut your mouth about things you don't understand, little girl."

She blinked her eyes. *Little girl. Okay?* "No, seriously Michael," She shifted uncomfortably on the floor. The zip ties brought on mild claustrophobia, and part of the plastic band on the outside was cutting into her skin. "He tried to do the same thing with me. Brent was the worst. He cornered me in the bank and tried to make me strike a deal with him."

He seemed to take a moment to think, which could have been good, could have been bad. But she had no other defenses. And she wasn't the type to cower in the corner or lose hope. She was a survivor. She hoped that Josie was on high alert. Surely Josie would look for her, since she hadn't come back from Michael's boutique to retrieve Robusta. She wouldn't just leave Robusta there. Sure, Josie had taken Robusta home for her before, but that was after Clem had agreed. Josie would look out the coffeehouse window and see that Michael's boutique looked closed. She might even try the door, see it locked, and hopefully alert someone. Clem glanced over at her phone on the floor of the cellar. It was face-down, and probably broken. It'd hit the floor when it fell from her pocket, and then was kicked across the room at a stone wall.

"What are you looking at!?" he shouted.

It startled her, and her whole body reacted, trembling at his voice. She tried to compose herself. "Nothing, I just looked at that wall over there."

When she looked back at Michael, standing between her and the stairs, some-thing caught her eye. She didn't know whether to stare or look away. At the top of the stairs, underneath the crack between the floor and the door, Clementine thought she saw a light turn off, then on again. She closed her eyes slowly and then opened them again. Had she imagined it? Was someone here?

It took everything inside her body to resist screaming for help. If there was nobody and she cried out, she was surely done for. Any progress she'd made getting him to delay his plans would have been shot. Not only that, but if someone was in the building, they wouldn't necessarily come in guns blazing. She'd heard nothing from upstairs, not a single creak in the floor, and these were old buildings. If there was someone sneaking around up there, they were definitely being strategic and quiet.

How would anyone know they were down here? There weren't many places to go inside the small boutique. When she took a calculated glance at her phone again, she noticed a wooden hatch-like door to the right of the stone wall. She'd seen that door before... only from the outside. She had been in the alley behind these buildings before. It wasn't on the same side of the street as the coffee shop, but she'd been back here once scouting solutions for parking and trash receptacles, two constant topics of contention at all of the community meetings—when they didn't have a large festival or town killings to discuss.

"Was that it—you owed him money?"

He scoffed. "None of your business."

"If you're planning to kill me, maybe it would feel good to finally tell someone? I know you've had to do a lot of hiding. And you know as well as anyone that that's nearly impossible to do in Roastwood Hollow." She had no idea how she'd been able to string any words into sentences. But, it was keeping her alive. Even if only for a second more.

The light flickered under the crack of the door again. Her eyes glazed. *No reaction. Do not show any reaction.* This time, instead of turning back off, it stayed on, glowing under the door just slightly.

"I don't understand Paul's murder, though. We were both his tenants. Was he a bad landlord to you?"

Michael heaved a large sigh. Was it from impatience and frustration, or had she struck a chord? "Also money?" she guessed.

"Alright, I'm done talking," he said point-edly, walking towards her and unscrewing the lid on the small container.

"Wait, wait!" she yelled out, pushing back with her feet on the floor. "Please just tell me one thing." She spoke louder this time, hoping that someone, anyone was within hearing distance. "Why Polly?" If she did one more thing before she was the next victim, it would be to clear her friend's name, even if only to her.

"Someone needed to be framed. It didn't work for you with Paul. But it did work with Polly for Brent."

"So… it was you who left the recording device in my roaster?" She threw in that thought, puzzle pieces coming together.

Michael smiled. "Now open wide—"

"Wait! Michael! There's a light on upstairs! Did you leave that light on?" She spoke as fast as the words could escape her lips.

His gaze jerked to the stairs. He stood there a moment. "I left it on. Right?"

"No, you turned it off when you closed the store." Clem tried to sound convincing. That wasn't a lie, regardless of the slight tremble in her voice.

"What the…" he said. He looked at her with an annoyed expression. But it had bought her a moment longer, because he recapped the vial and pocketed it. "If you even *think* about trying anything, Clementine…" He pointed in her face, his index finger centimeters away from her nose, her eyes going crossed.

She shook her head in response.

He started up the stairs one foot at a time,

stopping on each stair with his head turned to listen.

She sat stone cold on the floor. She likely wouldn't have time to run to the hatch door and somehow get it open without the use of her hands, since they were bound behind her back. If nobody was up those stairs, she would have made an effort. But wishful thinking had her banking on help. A glimmer of thought crossed her mind that she could be putting whoever was up there in danger. Didn't Michael lock the door? How could they, whoever they were, if there even was a they, even get inside?

Michael reached the top step.

Just as Clementine moved her legs behind her butt so that she could get better leverage to stand, the door to the basement burst open.

It knocked right into Michael, catching him by surprise and forcing him to stumble backwards down the stairs. He fell almost as if in slow motion. To Clementine, even in the swift commotion, she felt the satisfaction in her gut that he'd experienced the same fear he'd put her through moments before.

At the same time, bodies from the top of the basement stairs barreled down into the basement, and a bashing noise came from behind her. She tried to focus her eyes, realizing that police had come in from both the top of the stairs and the alley hatch door. They swarmed Michael, who was crumpled and stunned on the floor, at the moment he looked up to catch his bearings.

And at the head of the police raid...Officer Simon Drake.

CHAPTER
NINETEEN

Clementine watched it all happening in front of her like a blur, overwhelmed with emotion: relieved, exasperated, in shock.

He saved her.

Simon finished cuffing Michael and yanked him up from the ground. Michael winced, letting out a whine.

"Michael Cromley, you are under arrest for the murder of Paul Wright, the murder of Brent Wormwood, and the kidnapping and attempted murder of Clementine Matthews." He glanced over at her quickly, then back to his work.

Clementine's cheeks flushed and she sat, absorbing it all.

"What!? I didn't do that! What are you—"

"Oh, save it. You literally just confessed right before we bashed in the door. Widen your stance. Do you have anything on you that could hurt or poke me?"

He slumped his head and shook it.

Simon stood in front of Michael, face-to-face and at eye level. "I need a verbal response."

"No!" Michael shouted in disgust.

Clementine did not recognize Michael and his behavior. This was not the sweet, neighborly, boutique owner she'd worked around for years. She'd considered him her friend. They'd bonded on the platform of business ownership.

As she watched him take charge and pat Michael down, pulling the vial out of his pocket and handing it to another officer, Chief Brown came up behind her and placed a gentle hand on her shoulder. "Clem, I'm going to cut your zip ties, okay?" Her voice was kind.

Clem nodded, eyes welling. She didn't expect to get emotional from the sudden caring attention. She looked around the basement through blurry eyes. The entire Roastwood Hollow police force was in that basement and at the hatch door. She'd also heard footsteps above, meaning more first responders were in the building. She hadn't realized how much danger she was in when she walked into that boutique.

Her arms fell with instant burning relief when the chief cut the ties. She pulled her hands around to her chest and rubbed both wrists. It was only a short time she'd been bound, but both wrists felt raw. Luckily the band hadn't cut in enough to break the skin. She looked up at the chief and nodded in thanks.

"Can you stand?"

"Oh yeah." Clem confirmed, reaching for the hand that she put out.

She used Chief Brown's strength to pull up to her feet, realizing that her knees were trembling. "So you know it's not Polly?"

"Yes, we know. We'll explain all of that later. We're going to take you out this back door, okay?" She guided her that way.

Clem looked over her shoulder to the bottom of the stairs.

"Don't worry, he can't hurt anyone anymore." The chief said quietly as she ushered her through the hatch door and handed her off to two other officers.

Clem nodded again. "Thank you." Though when she'd looked back, she wasn't concerned with Michael's fate, nor did she not have confidence that the police force would take care of it for real this time.

She was looking at Simon. Surely the police would not typically allow a new officer to lead a case this big. She imagined him standing up and fighting to be on the front lines for her. She wanted to embrace him and thank him for not giving up; for listening to her concerns and not faltering. She watched him so concentrated on his work as she exited the building.

Clementine was ushered by policemen on either side as they trudged down the alley, away from the basement where she had been held captive and almost met the same fate as Paul and Brent. The night air was revitalizing. She celebrated her breath, visible in the chilly air. It reminded her that she was alive as they stumbled toward the ambulance at the end of the alley.

"Oh it's okay, I don't think I need that—"

One of the officers nodded to her legs. She looked down and saw that her thin jeans bore tears, gashes in her knees mixed with gravel. They must have braced her fall when she'd been pushed down the stairs. She hadn't even noticed. Drawing attention to them made her feel the sting. "Oh." She nodded, feeling the shock all over again.

Just as they reached the end of the alley, someone stepped into her peripheral vision. She jerked her head to see Josie's curly-haired head bouncing towards her, right before the embrace. She hugged her tight, the emotion that had been balled in her chest emerging again.

"I knew it! I knew you were in danger." Josie pulled back, staring Clem in the eyes, searching her face. "Are you okay, friend?" she asked.

Clem couldn't hide her small smile and nodded quickly. "I knew you'd save me," she said, right above a whisper.

"You would never leave Robusta and just go home. When I saw Made in The Hollow closed up and you hadn't come back, I knew right away."

Clem gave a small laugh. "I was hoping you wouldn't just take Robusta home, thinking I'd forgotten or got distracted or something."

"No, of course not. You also weren't answering your phone."

"My phone!" Clem breathed, looking over her shoulder down the alley.

"We'll recover it for you and have it at the station, Clem," one of the officers said. Clementine looked over at him; it was Todd, a guy she'd graduated high school with. Everyone truly did have a connection with everyone in Roastwood Hollow. She was so distracted before that she hadn't noticed. She nodded at him in thanks, then looked back at

Josie and saw Ryder standing behind her, grasping Robusta to his flannel.

"Robusta!"

Ryder instantly advanced, handing her Robusta and the leash from the harness. Clementine hugged Ro, resting her cheek on the bearded dragon's head.

"Hi ma'am, would it be all right if we took a look at your injuries?"

She opened her eyes to see the paramedic, gloved hands intertwined.

Josie and Ryder backed up for Clem to pass. The officers handed her off to the paramedic. Then one went back down the alley towards the basement, and the other walked up the street to round the front of the buildings.

"I'm going to head out. I'm glad you're okay, Clem!" Ryder said and waved, taking off back down the road.

"Do you want me to hold Robusta for you?" Josie asked her.

"I think I want to hold her a little longer." Clem smiled, keeping Ro close.

"Of course—here." Josie unraveled the handknit scarf from her neck and folded it like a blanket, pressing it onto Robusta.

Clementine took the scarf and kept the bearded dragon warm.

The paramedic led her over to the ambulance. "My name is Jamie, and I'll be taking care of you." He motioned for her to step up into the ambulance.

Josie backed up as though she were in the way, looking over her shoulder in the direction that Ryder took off. Clem took her spot on the gurney in the back of the ambulance, still holding Robusta as she sat down. "Josie? Will you stay too? Not sure I want to go home alone tonight."

Josie looked back at Clem. "Of course! I'd actually like that too. I need to go back to the shop and grab my things, but I'll hang out until you're ready."

Clementine nodded and looked back at the paramedic as he shined a light into both of her eyes.

"They say you were pushed down the stairs?"

She nodded.

"Did you hit your head at all, do you recall?"

She instinctively followed the light with her eyes back and forth for the paramedic.

"No, I landed on my hands and knees."

The paramedic looked down at her legs. "Oh right." He inspected her pants at the tattered knees. "Would you be okay if I cut these?" he asked. "I think it'd be much easier than pulling them up."

She nodded. "Can't be colder than it already is." She smiled.

He smiled in return. "Hey Terry, can you toss back that kit with the thermal blanket in it?" he called up to the paramedic sitting in the front seat. They shuffled up front and came between the seats, handing the blanket to Clem.

"Thank you," she said, taking the blanket and wrapping it around her shoulders. The cool metal of the shears brushed her skin as Jamie sliced into her thin, black jeans using the holes already made from her fall, just above the knee. "I've become something of a regular in this ambulance, huh?" She halfway joked, her tone light, but with an edge.

Jamie looked up at her over his glasses as he switched to the other leg. "Heroes need to be taken care of too."

Oof. Clementine felt that in the gut; her eyes stung again. "I'm no hero." She brushed off the comment and trained her gaze on Robusta's bumpy scales to refocus her mind. She was a closet crier. There would be no crying here in the ambulance tonight.

"I wouldn't expect a hero to say anything else," he half-smiled, inspecting both knees.

She sniffled. "I didn't save Paul or Brent. And I blamed my good friend, Polly, betraying her as well."

"It'll all work itself out. And don't blame yourself for the murders."

She shook her head.

He continued to talk while he worked. "You're a hero in more ways than one. You cared enough to keep fighting on. People in this town talk. Paramedics and police officers talk."

She had a sinking feeling he was talking about Simon. She didn't have time to ponder that before he went on.

"The rest of the town had moved on, making themselves comfortable with the familiarity of planning a festival to get everyone's mind off the murder—instead of uncovering the truth, like you did. Not only that, but you make something everyone in this town benefits from. You make people's day. You fuel first responders like myself to do our jobs. You are the reward that many people save for all week. You are important." He unscrewed the cap on a clear bottle of antiseptic and dabbed gauze on it, turning the bottle upside down to wet the gauze.

She absorbed what he said, her shoulders sinking. She hadn't realized how much she'd needed to hear that. It was nice to feel appreciated, and to be taken care of. She was so independent all the time, and in this moment, she could let go. Let her guard down. Relax, almost. That thought extinguished when he dabbed the gauze on her knee. The pain seared. She winced, trying not to move her leg.

"Good news is you don't need any repair work today. Just surface wounds. You must have hit that pavement pretty hard. I'd expect some soreness, but other than that I just need to finish cleaning the gravel out of your wounds and you should be good to go. When was your last tetanus shot?"

She wracked her brain. "A couple of years ago, actually. When we were moving the roaster over to the new building. A piece of the metal cut my thumb and I got one then."

"Ah, okay. They are good for ten years." He moved to the other knee.

Clem braced herself.

As he finished cleaning that one, he set the bottle and gauze down. "Can I see your hands and wrists real quick?"

She put her free hand out, facing it up. He gingerly grabbed and turned it, looking at both sides. "Just some redness, but looks okay."

She pulled it back and switched the hand that held Robusta. Then she gave him the other.

"I think you are looking good, Clem. I'd

recommend taking a NSAID, ibuprofen or Tylenol and you'll be good."

She nodded. "Thank you so much, Jamie. Truly."

"My pleasure." He smiled then turned and began to clean up. "Oh, you can keep the blanket. We get new ones all the time. Take your time getting out."

She nodded, then began to move, hopping off the bed and gingerly taking the stairs. The bare lower half of her legs were awkward in the open air.

"Would you like someone to walk with you back to the shop?" he asked over his shoulder.

"No, I'm okay. Thank you. Roastwood Hollow is the safest place to walk at night, right?" She saw a hint of a smirk on his face. She took off in the direction of the shop to meet up with Josie.

CHAPTER
TWENTY

The next day, Clementine got out of her car and brushed off her leggings, staring at her black Converse sneakers before straightening to see the police station. They had given her the night to rest and come down from her shock, but she'd been told that she needed to come to the station the next morning to make her statement.

She almost started walking towards the building before she remembered that she'd brought coffee for them. She rounded her car and pulled open the passenger side, careful not to ding the door of the police cruiser in the spot next to her, and picked up the cardboard carafe of fresh-roasted coffee. She knew not to walk into that police station without some kind of treat for them, and cops loved coffee. It was always a good decision to get on their good side; particularly because a part of her felt she'd get scolded for ignoring Simon's pleas for her to stop investigating. She hadn't —that much was clear to everyone now. She wasn't sure what the tone of this meeting would be.

The police station was attached to City Hall, and when she entered the lobby, the receptionist took the coffee graciously and pointed her to a hallway lined with doors to conference rooms.

She hesitated, then entered the conference room. Two officers sat in the chairs across the table. They both stood upon her entering, skidding their chairs back.

"Clem, how are you doing?" Simon asked.

Clementine smiled slightly, instantly relaxing at the familiarity, but also unsure how to gauge the mood of the room. "Yeah, I'm okay." She nodded, smiling courteously and pulling out the chair opposite them. "I brought coffee. Reception took it." She pointed at the door, then sat, the officers following suit.

"Thank you. Whatever you brought is without a doubt better than what we brew for ourselves here. I can guarantee that," the other officer joked. "I'm Captain Jones, from the Greater Roastwood Hollow County precinct, accompanying Officer Drake here, who I'm told you are acquainted with."

She nodded, shooting him a glance and then focusing back on Captain Jones. She was very familiar with who he was. She remembered him and his push-broom mustache from the night of Paul's murder at the roastery, not to mention his recent presence at the community meeting following the incident.

"We'd first like to get your statement on the events of last night, just to get the whole picture here. I understand this may not be an easy thing to do, so please feel free to take your time. Any and all details are important."

Clementine nodded. This was the easy part, honestly. She could recount the story. She'd had the night to get some rest, knowing that the real killer who had been terrorizing their small and comfortable town was put to justice. It had been the first real sleep she'd gotten in a long while. The first time she'd thought the killer had been caught, she'd had that sinking feeling that something wasn't quite right. And her intuition had been correct.

"… and that's when Sim—Officer Drake burst through the door and everyone came into the basement," she concluded, reaching for the paper cup on the table in front of her, placed there before she came in. The water in it coated her throat, soothing it.

"Thank you so much, Clementine," Captain Jones responded, finishing up a note he had been scrawling into his notebook on the table. He pushed back and stood up. "I'm going to check on this message I've received, but Officer Drake is going to finish up the interview and we will get you on your way. I apologize for what you've been through, Clementine, and I appreciate you for being an upstanding citizen and business owner here in Roastwood Hollow." He nodded, brushing over his bushy mustache with his hand. Then he grabbed his steno pad and left the room.

There was silence between the two of them as they sat across the table from each other. She looked up at Simon. She couldn't read the emotion on his face, but it felt natural to speak first. "Your dad must be so proud."

"Mm." He nodded, though his lips did not so much as twitch.

"I owe you an apology." The words left her lips before she had the opportunity to think about them. It was better that way.

"It doesn't matter anymore, Clem. You're safe," he said quietly.

It pierced her heart like a spear. She still didn't feel like what she did was wrong. But, she squirmed in guilt for betraying his trust.

"Are you still mad?" She sounded like a teenage girl asking it.

"I was never mad. I just wanted to protect you."

"I don't need protection," she said quietly, not sure if it was the best thing to say. "Ack, I'm sorry. Clearly, I needed you there at the end." She avoided his gaze.

"It's all in the past. I didn't avoid you or not answer your calls because I was upset. You have been an integral part of solving this case, actually. I've just been busy doing my job. I never for a second believed that Paul Wright's death was a suicide, nor that Brent's was cardiac arrest."

There was silence between them. "You were always one step ahead of me, huh?" she asked.

That comment made his lips twitch into a small smile. "I'd be a pretty terrible cop if I wasn't, right?"

She let out a small breathy chuckle.

"And if it weren't for you orchestrating the release of the voice recording, which was a welcome and unexpected surprise, we may have never caught the real killer."

"You knew it was me?"

"We had a hunch on Michael being the perpetrator, based on evidence found at Paul's crime scene… of which I cannot share all the details with you." He raised his eyebrow. "He must have known you were onto him and just couldn't resist framing Polly. And after you broadcasted the recording, it allowed us to stage Polly's arrest, which ultimately helped coax Michael out of the woodwork."

She was in awe. She really had no idea what had been going on in the background the whole time. And all those intrusive thoughts she'd had about the police not doing their jobs: she couldn't take any of that back. No sense dwelling on it.

"But Polly…" she whispered.

"She was our CI, Clem. Our informant."

Clementine was overwhelmed by that news. Polly was in on it the whole time. She was helping catch the bad guy. "She was acting the whole time she was arrested at the Snowflake Festival?" she asked in disbelief, just above a whisper, so many thoughts pouring into her mind.

"Staged. On a literal stage in front of the whole town, just the way we planned it," he concluded.

She wasn't sure whether she should be happy or feel duped. It had worked though, for everyone involved. And Polly, the one that gossiped the most and knew everyone and everything in this town, had put herself up on a pedestal to be ridiculed and talked about more than anyone. It was such a sacrifice, and a representation of her character.

Unless, of course, she knew that once her name was cleared… she'd be even more the talk of the town, and could easily repair any damage to her character. Clem always felt conflicted by Polly's motivation, if she was really her friend or just trying to drum up more gossip. And when it came to wondering if she was capable of murder, that was equally conflicting.

"That's…" She sighed and laughed in disbelief. "That is a lot to unpack there."

"Yes, and there is no need to rush it now." He pushed his chair back. "If you have no further questions for me or Captain Jones, then you are free to go. We really appreciate you coming in here and leaving your statement. Believe it or not, it really helps."

She nodded. How formal of him. However, they were in his place of work, and he was a professional.

"No other questions," she whispered, standing up and heading for the door, hesitantly.

"Oh, and thank you for the coffee!"

She looked over her shoulder at him and half smiled, nodded, then opened the door to the conference room. Her gaze trained on her shoes as she walked down the hall.

"Clementine?'

Her head jerked up, and her heart sank.

She stretched out her arms and embraced Polly in the stuffy, brown-carpeted hallway of the police station. "I'm so sorry," Clementine breathed into the shoulder of Polly's fuzzy pink sweater.

Polly gently pushed her back, holding her shoulders. "No, *I'm* sorry sweetie! So many secrets. I had to do it, you know?"

"I know that now. And of course you did," Clem said softly. "Thank you so much. Thank you for helping bring Paul," she swallowed, "and Brent's killer to justice. I'm still just in shock of who it was, you know?"

"Oh honey, I know. I feel the same way." She rubbed the side of Clem's arm. "You know how many times I was in that boutique alone with him? I thought nothing of it."

"Will you forgive me for throwing you under the bus?"

"You did what you thought was right with the resources you were given. Don't think anything of it."

"But you did have that heated conversation with Brent right before he died?"

She nodded. "I did. But I'm no killer. I was long gone out the front door before Michael slipped in from the kitchen side."

"Of course." Clem nodded.

"When the police were combing the office after Brent's murder, they found your bug."

"How did they know it was mine?"

"Well, for one, fingerprints, honey. And for two, they'd already bugged the office first and heard you and Josie in there."

Clem's cheeks rushed with warmth. One step ahead of her. "So the police were the ones who put the bug back in my roastery?"

"Well, they weren't expecting you to turn the machine back on." She laughed. "But Officer Drake had suspicions that you were poking around the case and thought he'd use it to his advantage."

Clem looked bashfully down at her shoes. "He wasn't wrong," she mumbled. Clem heaved a sigh of relief and looked at Polly with apologetic eyes. "I knew it wasn't you. Or I guess I should say, I was wishing it wasn't."

She smiled. "It's okay, Clem. Really." She swatted her hand as if to gesture it was no big deal. "Hey, we'll catch up more in a bit, sweetie." Then she turned and headed down the hall.

Clem clicked her tongue, stood in the hallway a moment longer as the conversation sunk in, and then took off down the opposite way.

CHAPTER
TWENTY-ONE

Clementine ran her hand along the stainless steel prep table to the end, where a pallet sat full of different burlap sacks of green coffee beans. She tugged on the corner burlap sack, one hundred and twenty pounds, pulling the sack taut to read the print on it.

It was from Guatemala, the Huehuetenango region. She loved to joke with customers to try to say that three times fast. It was a small three-generation women-owned farm. She'd done a video call with them and they showed her their entire operation. It wasn't so different from her own way of life, but also worlds away.

Clementine pulled open the top and reached in for a handful of beans. Beans cascaded over her palm as she brought it to her nose and took a large whiff. It smelled like bell peppers. Fresh, vegetal, like the soil of the country it was from. Nothing made her feel more connected. She dropped the beans back into the bag and grabbed her scale, a bucket, and a scoop to measure out the beans for the roaster, always the first step in the process.

As the roaster hummed through its pre-heat cycle, she reveled in the comfort of this craft, in this space. She couldn't wait to dive into the process of developing the beans and bringing out their best qualities, using the variables that she could control to manipulate the roast.

She thought about what Jamie, the paramedic, had said to her what felt like ages ago: that she was a hero for fueling his day with the caffeine he needed to save people. She never thought of her job as something noble and important. It was just something she enjoyed doing: the art and the science and the craft. But someone had told her how important she was. And just being important to one person was enough.

A purpose.

A calling.

Belonging.

As she went to check the temperature of the roaster, there was a knock at the door of the roastery. When she was in there by herself, which was most of the time, she always kept the door locked. The roaster was loud and she needed to be able to hear anyone coming in, of course. That's why she generally only opened it by appointment only.

She looked over to the door and saw Simon outside standing on the landing. Her stomach somersaulted. She was excited to see him. She was happy that they were able to re-connect at the police station, and that he had just been doing his job the entire time, not avoiding or ignoring or being angry with her. They'd just started to get to know each other, and it had already gone cold. She was happy to get to speak to him outside his professional environment—and that he sought that out as well.

She approached the door and opened it. "Hello, fancy seeing you here." She gestured for him to come inside. She pulled her fiery orange hair back into a ponytail and tied it.

Simon was wearing normal clothes, not his police uniform. A hunter green tee shirt, dark jeans, a black bomber jacket, and a navy blue beanie on his head to shield his ears from the chilled air.

He closed the door. For that she was grateful, because her bare arms caught the chill the moment before he shut it. She'd get warmed up soon enough being so close to the roaster. "I was just getting ready to throw in a batch."

"Can I help?" he asked.

She smiled, "Of course." She walked over to the shelves of tubs, pulled the denim apron off the hook, and put the strap around her neck, tying the other strap around her back. She pulled the other apron off the hook and walked it over to him.

Simon took the apron and followed suit.

"If you want, grab that bucket there and charge the beans—uh, pour the beans up inside the hopper, this funnel right here—" She reached up and pointed to the hopper, careful not to touch it because of the heat.

He listened, stretched his arms above his head, and poured the beans into the funnel of the roaster.

She smiled. "Usually I need a step stool for that, so it's nice to have an assistant that can pour them in without it."

He laughed. Once he loaded the roaster with the beans, Clem pulled the lever and charged the coffee, simultaneously setting a timer as well. She stood back a moment, looking him over. They had about six minutes before the first airflow change in the roast. "I'm glad you're here," she said softly. "After everything."

He nodded. "I'm glad you're here too. That must have been terrifying in that basement."

She thought for a moment, and then shrugged, even though he was correct.

"Clementine?" He fidgeted his foot, swinging it back and forth a moment before settling.

"Hm?" *Here we go…* she thought. He's going to say he can't be around her anymore or that he was being moved to a different precinct or something else.

"I was wondering if you'd like to go on an actual date… with me. Get food or do something normal people do, like mini golf or something."

She laughed.

"What? Should I not have…"

"No, no. I'm just laughing in disbelief because I thought that you were going to say the opposite: that you were leaving or that you couldn't see me anymore."

"Oh, no. Well, not yet anyway. I'll be here in Roastwood a little while longer at least."

She looked at the temperature of the roaster and wrote down the turn point, the moment when the temperature began to rise again after pouring in cold beans. "I would like that." She looked at him with a small smile. "I would like to get to know who you are when we're not both in …intense situations."

"But… like a date where it's just me and

you… not me, you, and Josie. I mean, I like Josie and all but…"

She laughed heartily. "Yeah, sorry. I didn't know you! I didn't know you wanted it to be just us. It was weird."

"It's okay." He recovered. "I'm just teasing. But… also not."

"Right." Her cheeks started to ache from smiling so much.

"Are you ready for the first airflow change?" she asked. "Come over here, I'll show you where to move the lever to."

Simon did not hesitate and moved around the roaster to meet her on the same side. "As long as there's coffee to drink at the end of this."

"Oh, you can always count on that," she responded as she reached for the trier to sample the beans. The roast continued to spin in the drum, the airflow changing at their hand from cooling, to fifty-fifty, to roasting. The vapors of the batch moved around the roaster, out the back of the machine, up the ducting, through the chimney in the roof, and out into the cool winter air.

The smell of freshly roasted coffee wafted through the cobblestone streets of Roastwood Hollow.

❄

IF YOU ENJOYED THIS READ, PLEASE LEAVE A REVIEW!

THEN MARK YOUR CALENDAR FOR THE NEXT ROASTWOOD HOLLOW FESTIVAL...

Breweries from all over the region come to take part in Roastwood Hollow's annual Brew Bash Festival. Coffee Roaster, Clementine Matthews uses this opportunity to debut her well thought out cold brew recipe. With the chaos of the festival and the already short-staffed local police focused elsewhere, a body is found on a trail in the park nearby. Little did she know that instead of cold brew, she'd be dealing with a cold-blooded murderer.

ABOUT THE AUTHOR

Kristin Helling writes thrillers and cozy mysteries. When she's not killing people (fictionally, of course!), she also has a passion for children's stories and writes them under the pen name Kristin Alis.

Kristin owns a coffeehouse, co-owns the publishing imprint Wordwraith Books, is married to a Photographer, and is Mama of two.

Her drink of choice depends on the day: Single origin. Cortado. Caramel drizzle latte. London fog.

More from Kristin Helling here: www.kristinhelling.com

Made in the USA
Monee, IL
28 February 2025